An Actress Has to Make Sacrifices . . .

Jessica settled back on her bed and began to read the script. It was really funny.

Jessica's eyes widened. She could hardly believe what she had just read. It couldn't be! It was just too horrible for words!

"Elizabeth!" Jessica cried as she jumped off her bed and flew downstairs.

Elizabeth was in the kitchen when Jessica raced in. "This is awful!" Jessica cried. "It's disgusting! It's repulsive! We can't have this in the movie!"

"Can't have what?" Elizabeth asked.

"We can't have this," Jessica cried frantically, pointing to the script. "This . . . this kiss!"

Elizabeth smiled. "Why? What's wrong with it?"

"You know very well what's wrong with it," Jessica retorted. "Kissing Winston Egbert, that's what's wrong with it!"

Bantam Skylark Books in the SWEET VALLEY TWINS AND FRIENDS series
Ask your bookseller for the books you have missed

SWEET VALLEY TWINS
AND FRIENDS

The Slime
That Ate
Sweet
Valley

◇

Written by
Jamie Suzanne

Created by
FRANCINE PASCAL

A BANTAM SKYLARK BOOK
NEW YORK · TORONTO · LONDON · SYDNEY · AUCKLAND

RL 4, 008–012

THE SLIME THAT ATE SWEET VALLEY
A Bantam Skylark Book / October 1991

Sweet Valley High® and Sweet Valley Twins and Friends are
trademarks of
Francine Pascal

Conceived by Francine Pascal

Produced by Daniel Weiss Associates, Inc.
33 West 17th Street
New York, NY 10011

Cover art by James Mathewuse

Skylark Books is a registered trademark of Bantam Books, a division of
Bantam Doubleday Dell Publishing Group, Inc.
Registered in U.S. Patent and Trademark Office and elsewhere.

ISBN 0-553-15935-6

Published simultaneously in the United States and Canada

Bantam Books are published by Bantam Books, a division of Bantam
Doubleday Dell Publishing Group, Inc. Its trademark, consisting of
the words "Bantam Books" and the portrayal of a rooster, is Registered
in U.S. Patent and Trademark Office and in other countries. Marca
Registrada. Bantam Books, 666 Fifth Avenue, New York, New York
10103.

PRINTED IN THE UNITED STATES OF AMERICA

OPM   0 9 8 7 6 5 4 3 2 1

To Sara Elizabeth Dyson

One

◇

"I need a break!" Jessica Wakefield moaned.

Jessica's twin sister Elizabeth pulled her English book out of her locker and shut the door. "But today's only Monday. We just *had* a break."

"Right, Jess," Todd Wilkins said. "Isn't a weekend long enough?"

Jessica flipped her long blond hair over her shoulder. "Definitely not," she said. "What I mean is that I need a break in the *routine*. Aren't you fed up with it, too? Ever since school started, we've done nothing but work, work, work. I'm tired of teachers and sick of classes. I'm ready to have some *fun!*"

"Jess," Elizabeth teased, "you're *always* ready to have some fun."

"Yeah," Todd agreed. "Fun is your middle name!"

Jessica laughed at how well Elizabeth knew her. She *was* always ready for a good time. The two were identical twins, but other than their long blond hair, their sparkling blue-green eyes, and the dimple each had in her left cheek, they were not very much alike at all. Jessica loved to hang out with her friends in the Unicorns, an exclusive club of the prettiest and most popular girls at Sweet Valley Middle School. Jessica and the Unicorns spent their time shopping at the Sweet Valley Mall, going to parties, and talking on the phone about boys, clothes, and their favorite stars.

Elizabeth was the older twin, by four minutes, and the more responsible of the two. Her friends were the kids she worked with on *The Sweet Valley Sixers*, the sixth-grade newspaper she had helped start. She was good at her schoolwork, and she enjoyed reading mysteries written by Amanda Howard. But most of all, Elizabeth loved to write. She had recently been named Junior Journalist by the Sweet Valley *Tribune*, and the magazine *Teen Scene* had given her essay on being an individual first prize in its national essay contest. But for all her seriousness and sense of responsibility, Elizabeth liked to have fun, too, especially with her best friend, Amy Sutton, and her boyfriend, Todd Wilkins.

"Well, Jess," Elizabeth continued, "I guess I know what you're talking about. It seems that lately there's been one huge homework assignment after another."

"Yeah," Todd said. "First there was that big social studies project, then the science project. What next?"

Jessica frowned. "All work and no play makes a *very* dull person!"

"And speaking of dull," Todd added, "I'd better get to math class. Hang in there, Jess. See you Elizabeth." Todd waved and walked off.

When Jessica and Elizabeth got to English class, Mr. Bowman was standing in front of the room holding up a rubber snake.

"Who put this snake on my seat?" he asked, looking around with an exaggerated scowl.

The class laughed.

"I'm afraid you have been working too hard," Mr. Bowman continued. "Your minds have snapped." The class laughed even louder.

"Hey, it's not funny," Mr. Bowman protested. "It's true—your brains are turning to mush. Those essays you wrote last week were awful! They've got so many red marks on them, they look like they've been dipped in Kool-Aid. And the same thing is true in the other sixth-grade English classes. What's going on?"

Jessica raised her hand. "If our brains are turning to mush," she said, "maybe it's because we've been doing too much reading and writing. Maybe we should do something else for a change—something *fun*."

"Maybe you're right, Jessica," Mr. Bowman answered. "Anybody have any ideas for ways to liven things up, for this class as well as the other sixth-grade classes I teach?"

After a moment, Winston Egbert raised his hand.

"We could do oral interviews," he suggested, "like we did for history class."

"You mean, interview our grandmothers *again*?" Charlie Cashman asked. "Hey, no way, man!"

"We could write biographies about our favorite stars," Jessica said. "At least the research would be fun."

But Jerry McAllister shouted, "No more writing!" and the rest of the class nodded.

Then Leslie Forsythe raised her hand. "We could make a movie," she suggested timidly.

Jessica looked over at Leslie and saw that she was blushing. Leslie was thin and very shy. Just now her huge black eyes looked like they were swallowing her face. Her dark hair was very long, a little *too* long, Jessica thought. She hardly ever spoke unless she was called upon, and she never made an effort to make friends. As far as Jessica knew, she had called attention to herself only once before, when she had recently supported Winston in his efforts to join the Boosters.

"A movie?" Jessica asked.

"A *movie!*" Lila Fowler exclaimed excitedly. "Why didn't I think of that?"

"What made you think of suggesting a movie, Leslie?" Mr. Bowman asked.

"Well, making a movie would be educational," Leslie said eagerly. "It would involve lots of careful planning and organizing. Somebody has to write a script, somebody has to direct—"

"We'd need actors and camera people, too," Randy Mason said unexpectedly. Jessica turned to look at Randy and caught him pushing his glasses up on his nose. Like Leslie, he had supported Winston's bid to be a Booster, which had only confirmed the Unicorns' opinion of him as a nerd.

A particularly sore spot for Jessica was the fact that Randy had defeated her in the race for sixth-grade president. While she had to admit that Randy had many good ideas for the sixth grade, being elected president had not made him any less nerdy.

"We'd also need film editors and costume designers," Caroline Pearce added eagerly. "And a prop manager and—" Caroline reached for her notebook. "I'll make a list of all the jobs that need to be filled."

"Hold it, hold it," Mr. Bowman interrupted.

"Let's not get carried away. Movie-making is a big-budget business. What makes you think our English classes can afford it?"

"We wouldn't need a big budget if we used a video camera," Elizabeth replied. "Videotape doesn't cost very much. And if we used a camcorder, we could look at the film as we go along, without having to wait for it to be developed. We could use the VCR that we got for the library with our book fair money."

"Yeah," Pete Stone said excitedly. "And the library's got a camcorder we could borrow. Our science class used it once."

Mr. Bowman looked approvingly at the class. "Now that we've started talking about movies, your minds seem to have turned from mush into minds again. So does everyone think the sixth-grade English classes should make a movie?"

"Yes!" everybody shouted.

Mr. Bowman grinned. "Well, I guess you've talked me into it. Since you're all so eager, let's make a movie—starting tomorrow. But today, oral reports."

Everybody groaned.

"I know," Mr. Bowman said sympathetically. "You probably want to start shooting today. But as Caroline said, we've got a lot of planning to do first. For one thing, we have to decide what *kind* of a movie we're going to make."

"I vote for a love story," Lila said promptly.

"Save your ideas for tomorrow, Lila," Mr. Bowman said as he took out his grade book. "We'll decide then what kind of movie we're going to make. But today, oral reports. Elizabeth, we'll start with you."

While Elizabeth got up in front of the class to give her report on Mark Twain, Jessica sat back in her seat and began to think. She had wanted a break in the routine and now she had gotten one, thanks to Leslie's terrific idea. Best of all, when the class got around to choosing the actors for their movie, Jessica knew that *she* would be chosen to be the star. She had more acting experience than anybody else in the sixth-grade—except for Maria Slater, who used to be a child actress in Hollywood. But Jessica hoped that Maria would be too busy with the Drama Club to take on another role right now. With all her experience and her natural ability, Jessica knew that she would be everyone's first choice.

After class, Lila and Ellen Riteman stopped at Jessica's desk. "Isn't it terrific?" Jessica said. "We're going to make a movie, and *I'm* going to get the lead."

"*You* will!" Lila exclaimed disbelievingly. "What makes you think *you'll* get the lead?"

Ellen laughed. "It's because she's finally gotten rid of those dorky glasses!" For a while, Jessica had had to wear glasses to correct a minor vision problem. Just last week the doctor had said her eyes were fine.

"No. It's because I'm the most talented," Jessica retorted. "Did you forget that I once starred with Dolores Dufay, one of the most famous actresses of *all time*?"

"Don't you think Dolores Dufay is a little out-of-date?" Lila asked haughtily. "And I don't know what makes you think you're the *only* star material around here. Other people have acting talent, too, you know." Lila tossed her head and walked off, followed by Ellen.

Jessica looked after her best friend and shook her head pityingly. *Poor Lila*, she thought. *It's obvious she has her heart set on the starring role. She'll be so disappointed when she doesn't get it!*

To Leslie Forsythe's surprise, she found herself the center of attention after English class.

"That was a great idea you had, Leslie," Elizabeth said, as they headed for their next class.

"Yeah," Amy Sutton said. "Making a movie is going to be really *fun*."

"Now all we have to do," Brooke Dennis said, "is figure out what kind of movie we want to make. What do you think, Leslie?"

Leslie hesitated. "I'd like to hear your ideas

first," she answered shyly. "Elizabeth, what do *you* think?"

"Well, we could make a movie using the plot of Amanda Howard's latest mystery," Elizabeth suggested. "But it might be too complicated," she added.

"Since this is our first movie," Leslie said quietly, "we probably need a story with a pretty simple plot and not too many characters."

"OK. We could make a movie about a baton twirler, and I could be the star!" Amy suggested with a laugh.

"Yeah, and Winston could be your co-star," Sophia Rizzo teased. "After all, he is the newest and hottest member of the Boosters."

Leslie giggled. "Did you know that Lila and Jessica tried to bribe me not to sign Winston's petition? They promised they'd wave at me when they saw me in the hallway if I didn't."

Elizabeth rolled her eyes. "The Unicorns are totally impossible!"

"We could make a movie about a rock band," Brooke suggested. "You know, a rockumentary. My dad could probably help us find a band to star in it. He's got a lot of connections in the music industry."

"But don't you think *we* should be the stars?" Leslie asked tentatively.

"Yeah, you're right," Brooke agreed.

"Maybe we should make a list of all the movies we really like," Elizabeth said, "and see if there's a theme or story we all agree on."

Leslie hesitated a moment before speaking. "I don't know if this will help, but I have a friend named Deirdre who knows everything there is to know about movies. She's the manager of Sweet Valley Video."

"I've been there," Elizabeth said. "That's where we always rent our movies."

"Deirdre studied acting at UCLA," Leslie added.

"Wow," Brooke said. "Dad says they have a great acting program."

Leslie nodded. "That's what Deirdre says, too. She's taught me a lot about movies and acting. Sometimes I go over to Sweet Valley Video after school. She puts a movie in the VCR and we watch it and talk about it."

"Deirdre sounds like just the person we need to know," Elizabeth said enthusiastically.

"Why don't we go over there this afternoon after school?" Leslie suggested.

"It's a deal," Elizabeth said.

Leslie smiled. She could not remember when she had felt more at ease around other kids. And she could not remember when she had talked so much without first worrying about what she was going to say!

Two

◇

After school, Elizabeth, Amy, Brooke, and Sophia went to meet Leslie at her locker. On the way, they ran into Maria Slater.

"Hi, Maria," Elizabeth said. "We're going over to Sweet Valley Video with Leslie to get some ideas about what kind of movie to make. Want to come?"

"I can't," Maria said. "I'm on my way to Drama Club practice."

"You're going to try out for the female lead in our movie, aren't you?" Amy asked. "I mean, with all your movie and TV experience, you're sure to get the part."

"No, I don't think I can," Maria said. "The Drama Club is taking up a lot of my free time. But I'd really like to help with the scriptwriting."

Maria grinned. "Anyway, I'll bet Jessica's got her eye on the lead."

"Not just Jessica," Sophia said. "I heard Lila tell Ellen that *she* was going to land the lead, and that she'd do *anything* to get it."

"I don't think a little competition will worry Jessica!" Maria glanced at her watch. "Gotta go, you guys. I'll see you later."

Elizabeth and the others waved and continued on their way. "You know," Amy said thoughtfully, "I was kind of surprised that Leslie talked to us after class. I don't think I'd heard her say more than two or three words before this morning."

"She's awfully shy," Brooke said. "But she seems really nice."

"Yeah, and she seems to know a lot about movies," Elizabeth said. "And if Deirdre knows as much as Leslie says she does, we'll have a great afternoon!"

Leslie looked worriedly at her watch. Elizabeth and her friends had said they would meet her at her locker right after school. What if they had changed their minds and forgotten to tell her? What if—

"Hi, Leslie," Elizabeth called out. "Sorry we're late, but we ran into Maria Slater."

"Deirdre and I watched one of Maria's movies

last week—*Party Girl*," Leslie said. "Have you guys seen it? Lanny Howard co-starred as her brother—remember him? He was also in *Last Chance for the Rainbow*. Maria had a small part in that movie, too." Leslie bit her lip. "Oops," she said with a nervous laugh. "I didn't mean to monopolize the conversation."

"No way! You know a *lot* about movies, Leslie," Sophia said respectfully.

"Really," Brooke agreed.

"Well, I just pay attention," Leslie said quickly. "Anyway, wait until you meet Deirdre. She know *lots* more than I do."

"Then what are we waiting for?" Elizabeth asked. "Let's go!"

Leslie always loved going to Sweet Valley Video. The brightly lit store was full of racks and racks of movies to rent in all different categories—dramas, comedies, Westerns, mysteries, documentaries, and old classics. The walls were covered with posters advertising the latest releases. Sometimes Leslie spent hours browsing through the store's collection before she decided on a movie to rent.

Leslie also loved to go to Sweet Valley Video because her secret fantasy was to be an actress. But Leslie was far too shy to ever do anything about it!

Today, Leslie headed straight for the counter

at the back of the store, the other girls trailing behind her. Deirdre was standing behind the counter, and she smiled when she saw Leslie approach. Leslie thought Deirdre was very cool and very beautiful. Her long auburn hair was always loosely pulled back, and she usually wore long sweaters over black stirrup pants.

"Hi, Les," Deirdre said. She smiled at the other girls. "I see you've brought some friends."

"Deirdre, I'd like you to meet Elizabeth, Brooke, Amy, and Sophia. Everyone, this is Deirdre McDaniel."

"It's nice to meet you," Deirdre said. "Are you girls looking for a special movie?"

"Actually," Leslie said, "we're planning to *make* a movie."

"Our English teacher at Sweet Valley Middle School was looking for a project for all of his sixth-grade classes, and Leslie suggested making a movie," Elizabeth explained.

"Now all we have to do is figure out what kind of movie we want to make," Amy added. "Leslie thought we might be able to get some ideas here."

"Why don't you browse around and find some films you like?" Deirdre suggested. "Then we can talk about why you like them and see what it is you're all really interested in."

Chattering excitedly, the girls scattered through the store. Leslie stayed behind at the counter.

Deirdre grinned. "A movie, huh? Are you going to audition for the lead?"

Leslie felt herself getting red. "Oh, I wouldn't stand a chance," she said with a shrug. "There are a couple of other girls in our class with lots of acting experience. Like Maria Slater and Jessica Wakefield. She once played opposite Dolores Dufay."

"There's a first time for everybody," Deirdre said. She leaned on the counter and looked seriously at Leslie. "This movie sounds like your perfect first time, Leslie. Don't let yourself miss out on it." Deirdre smiled. "And remember, the movie was *your* idea."

"I didn't bring up the idea of making a movie so that I could star in it," Leslie said quickly.

"Of course not," Deirdre replied. "But I still think you should auditon."

Leslie nodded, but she promised nothing. How could she confess to Deirdre that just the *idea* of auditioning gave her stage fright? And being in front of a camera could only be worse. Leslie hurried away to join Elizabeth and the others.

"Listen to these ideas," Elizabeth said about an hour later, when the girls had regrouped. She looked at the notes she had taken. "We could make a sad movie about a boy who finds a lost dog, or an inspiring movie about a girl who wins a skating competition."

"Or a historical movie," Amy added. "One that takes place during the California Gold Rush."

"Or a spoof," Brooke said. "Anyway, a comedy would be more fun to make than a serious movie."

"Remember that what sort of movie you make will depend on a lot of practical things," Deirdre said. "Like how much money you have for props and costumes, and how much time you have, and how much effort you want to put into sets and special effects and background music." She glanced at Leslie. "It also depends on how much creative talent you have in the class—actors, scriptwriters and directors."

"Wow," Sophia said, "I didn't know it was so complicated."

"Complicated but fun," Deirdre replied. "So are you going to invite me to your world premiere?"

"Sure thing!" Leslie said enthusiastically.

"Deirdre is really super," Elizabeth said to Leslie as they were leaving the store.

"Yeah," Amy said. "No wonder you like her. Mr. Bowman is really going to be impressed with all the fantastic ideas we've got."

"Maybe *he* will," Brooke said. "But some of

the other kids aren't going to be so impressed with all of our ideas."

"What do you mean?" Sophia asked.

"The Unicorns are set on making a love story," Brooke explained. "I heard them talking about it at lunch. And their plot sounded like a stupid soap opera!"

"And the guys want to make a horror film," Amy said. "Jim Sturbridge and Charlie Cashman were talking about it this afternoon in the library." Amy grinned. "Actually, a horror movie might be kind of fun."

"Between the boys and the Unicorns, we'll probably spend most of tomorrow's class arguing," Sophia said.

"Hey, I've got the perfect solution to the argument," Elizabeth said. "We'll make a comic spoof of a horror-story plot with a love-story ending!"

"Fantastic!" Amy said. "An idea with something for everyone!"

Jessica could hardly wait for English class to begin the next morning. Today might be the day she got the female lead in the class movie. But Jessica was disappointed.

"Some of you were asking about auditions earlier," Mr. Bowman said when the class had gathered. "Auditions won't be held until Thursday. Before we can choose actors, we have to know what kind of movie we're going to make and what parts we have to fill. It's up to you to come up with some ideas, which I'll pass on to my other sixth-grade classes. When we've got a consensus, we can begin to audition."

Thursday! Jessica thought. *That's two whole days away!*

"The guys want to make a horror movie," Charlie announced. "The more horrible, the better."

"Yeah," Jerry said. "With vampires and blood, and skeletons in the corners, and little weird green things crawling around, and lots of spooky spiders and bats hanging from the ceiling."

"And special sound effects," Pete added as he leaned over and grated his fingernails across the side blackboard.

"Vampires and weird green things are totally repulsive," Lila said firmly.

"Yeah, repulsive," Ellen agreed. "The girls want to make a love story, Mr. Bowman."

"A love story?" Mr. Bowman asked. "What kind of plot do you have in mind?"

Ellen spoke excitedly. "Well, there's this very pretty girl, see, and she gets really sick, and her boyfriend swears that he'll never leave her, and the doctors say—"

Charlie put his hands to his mouth and made a loud gagging noise. "Talk about repulsive! Who wants to watch a stupid old soap opera with a bunch of hugging and kissing!"

Jessica glared at Charlie. "Hugging and kissing is better than grossing everybody out with blood and vampires," she said indignantly. "At least we'll be appealing to our viewers' higher natures."

Elizabeth raised her hand. "How about a movie about a boy and a dog?"

Jessica frowned at Elizabeth. A boy and a dog? Was her sister kidding? That would mean a *boy* would have the lead!

"Or a movie about a girl who wins a skating competition?" Amy suggested.

"Or a movie about the Gold Rush," Sophia said.

"I still think it should be a love story," Lila insisted.

"Maybe we could work a love story into the plot about a girl who wins the skating competition," Jessica suggested, suddenly remembering that she was a much better skater than Lila.

"I don't think skating is a good idea at all," Lila retorted coldly.

Jerry folded his arms across his chest. "It's got to be a horror movie," he said.

"How about combining love and horror in a spoof?" Elizabeth suggested.

"That sounds like a good idea," Randy said.

"A spoof?" Jessica asked doubtfully. "How do you spoof a love story?" She was not at all sure she liked the idea of playing the lead role in a *comedy*.

"Well, it's better than no love story at all," Lila admitted. "Anyway, we've got to agree on *something*."

After another ten minutes of discussion, the class finally agreed to combine a horror story and a love story in a comedy. If the other sixth graders agreed, it would be up to the scriptwriters to come up with a story.

"Now that we've got a possible theme," Mr. Bowman said, "we need to come up with a list of the positions we'll need to fill." As the class suggested jobs, he wrote them on the board. The list included camera people, actors, film editors, a prop manager, a costume designer, set builders, and a special effects manager.

Suddenly Jessica heard a funny noise, like a cricket chirping. It stopped when Mr. Bowman turned around to face the class, and it started again when he turned back to the board. Out of the corner of her eye, Jessica saw that Pete Stone had one of his hands in his pocket.

Mr. Bowman turned around again. "Is it my imagination," he asked, "or is there a cricket in the room?" Everybody looked around the room, but no one answered. Jessica glanced quickly at Pete, who winked at her. She tried not to smile.

"Maybe our phantom cricket will volunteer for a job on our sound team," Mr. Bowman said dryly. The cricket chirped three times in response, then was silent. Jessica saw Pete take his hand out of his pocket.

Mr. Bowman stepped back and pointed to the board. "OK, back to business. That's the complete list," he said. "Tonight I want everyone to think about what he or she would like to do. Now we have to make another decision. Do we want to show our movie to the rest of the school?"

"I think we should have an open showing for the seventh and eighth grades," Elizabeth said.

"We could invite our families, too," Leslie said.

"Yeah," Charlie added. "And we could sell popcorn and candy, like a real movie theater."

"We could invite the movie reviewer from the Sweet Valley *Tribune*," Lila suggested.

"Good idea, Lila," Mr. Bowman said. "Every movie deserves to be reviewed." Jessica rolled her eyes. Obviously, Lila was expecting the paper to write a rave review of *her* lead performance.

Just then the bell rang. "That's it for today," Mr. Bowman said. "Don't forget—auditions will be held Thursday!"

*   *   *

"What's on your mind, Jessica?" Mrs. Wakefield asked as she sat down to dinner. "You seem a little preoccupied."

"I was just thinking about the movie we're making in English class," Jessica explained. "It's partly a love story, and I'm going to audition for the lead. I'm sure I'll get it, too."

Mrs. Wakefield smiled at Mr. Wakefield. "It's hard to believe that we have a daughter old enough to have the lead in a love story, isn't it, Ned?"

Mr. Wakefield grinned at Jessica and Elizabeth. "It is a bit scary," he agreed.

Jessica nodded. "Well, now that I'm twelve, I really have to start thinking seriously about my professional acting career. I mean, look at Maria Slater. She's twelve, and she's already made a *ton* of movies."

Steven, the twins' fourteen-year-old brother, laughed loudly. "Maria Slater is a pro," he said. "What makes you think you're going to take the lead away from her?"

"For your information, Mr. Know-It-All," Jessica retorted, "Maria isn't even trying out. She's too busy with the Drama Club. Which leaves the lead open for me!"

"What are you going to do in the movie, Elizabeth?" Mrs. Wakefield asked.

"I'd like to be a scriptwriter," Elizabeth replied.

"What kind of a movie are you making?" Mr. Wakefield asked as he poured gravy on his mashed potatoes.

"It's a combination horror story, love story, comedy," Elizabeth explained.

"Sounds like quite a combination," Mr. Wakefield said with a chuckle. "Is this amazing epic for a private audience only, or does the public get to see it?"

"Oh, no, we're going to have a showing for our families and friends. Please come and see it, Dad," Jessica begged. "You'll come too, won't you Mom?"

"When is it?" Mrs. Wakefield asked.

"Probably in about two weeks," Elizabeth said. "It'll take us at least that long to make it."

"I'm sure we'll still be here," Mr. Wakefield said.

"Still be here?" Elizabeth asked. "Are you going somewhere?"

Mrs. Wakefield smiled. "As a matter of fact, we are," she said. "Your father and I are thinking of going to Mexico for a week. But it's still tentative," she added.

"Mexico!" Jessica cried. "Can I come too?"

"No!" Mr. Wakefield said. "This is a trip just for your mother and me. You kids are staying home."

"But who will stay with us?" Elizabeth asked.

"We don't need anybody to stay with us!" Jessica said emphatically. "We're old enough to stay by ourselves. I mean, if I'm old enough to star in a movie, I'm certainly old enough to take care of myself for a week!"

Steven nodded. "I'm with Jessica," he said. "We're too old for a baby-sitter."

"Well, there's plenty of time to discuss that issue," Mr. Wakefield said. "The important thing is that we'll be in Sweet Valley for the movie."

"Your dad's right," Mrs. Wakefield said. "Neither of us can resist a good horror movie!"

"It sounds very resistible to me," Steven said. "Especially with you as the star, Shrimp."

"When I'm a famous movie actress, Steven," Jessica said coldly, "you will *eat* every single one of those words."

Steven laughed. "When you're a famous movie actress, I think I'll lose my appetite!"

Jessica sat back in her chair and glared at Steven. Her brother was such a pain. And so stupid, too. He couldn't even recognize true talent when it sat right across the table from him!

When dinner was over, Jessica and Elizabeth began clearing the table. "I know you want the movie to be a love story," Elizabeth said. "But I'm sure you'll make a good comic actress, Jess.

Remember how good you and Mandy were in the vaudeville skits?"

"We were fabulous. But I'd make an even better romantic actress." Jessica sighed dramatically. "I wish Aaron would audition for the male lead. It would be so *wonderful* to play opposite him! I can see it now. When the big love scene comes at the end, he'd sweep me into his arms and smother me with kisses! I just know he'd make a perfect romantic hero!"

"He'd have to swallow his bubble gum first," Steven said as he peeked into the room. Jessica threw a leftover roll at him, and he ran off.

"Isn't Aaron going to audition?" Elizabeth asked as they took the dishes into the kitchen.

"No," Jessica replied. "He wants to work with the music. You know how he likes to fool around with his stereo."

"Well, I think the right theme music is just as important as good acting," Elizabeth said.

"I don't think I'd go *that* far," Jessica protested. "If we don't have good acting, the movie will be a flop!"

Just then the phone rang, and Jessica ran to answer it. "It's probably Aaron!" she yelled.

But it was Todd. As Jessica handed the phone to her sister, she frowned. If Aaron Dallas were going to be a real romantic hero, the first thing he would have to do is start calling her more often!

In class on Wednesday, Mr. Bowman handed everybody a sheet of paper.

"The other English classes think your idea for the movie is terrific," he said. "So today we choose jobs. Please list your first, second, and third choices. Everybody but the lead actors will have more than one job."

Jessica sat staring at her form, and then at the list of jobs still written on the board, trying to decide what other jobs she could tolerate if the impossible happened and she did not get the female lead. Finally she glanced across the aisle at Lila. Lila had written only one word on all three lines of her form: actress, actress, actress. The letters were so big that they could be seen halfway across the room. Jessica had the feeling that that was what Lila had intended.

Jessica set her lips together firmly and wrote actress, actress, actress on her own form. Now if she didn't get the female lead, she would probably end up stuck on the clean-up crew or something equally gross. *But I will get the lead role, Jessica told herself fiercely. I have to get it! I can't let Lila Fowler beat me out of it!*

Suddenly there was a crash, and Jessica nearly jumped out of her skin. An easel in the corner of the room nearest Pete's seat had fallen over.

"The ghost of the English classroom strikes again," Mr. Bowman said dryly.

"Hey, that's not a bad idea!" Jerry said. "We could call our movie *The Ghost of Sweet Valley Middle School.* It could be about this kid who gets killed. . . ."

"He gets poisoned in the cafeteria," Winston said. "He chokes to death on contaminated spaghetti!"

"Yeah," Jerry said eagerly. "And then he comes back to haunt the school."

"Who would want to haunt a stupid school?" Charlie asked. "If I came back to haunt, I'd haunt the cheerleading squad!"

As Mr. Bowman went over to pick up the easel, Jessica spotted Pete reeling in a long piece of string. Mandy saw it, too, and leaned over to Jessica.

"Hey, *Pete*'s the ghost!" she whispered.

"Yeah," Jessica whispered back. "He was making the cricket noise yesterday, and I'll bet he was the one who put the snake on Mr. Bowman's chair. But don't tell. There's no point getting Pete into trouble."

"I won't. I think he's funny," Mandy replied.

"OK," Mr. Bowman said, gathering up all the forms just as the bell rang. "Tomorrow I'm going to bring a classic horror film to class for us to study." He raised his voice over the noise of scraping chairs. "Auditions will be tomorrow after school, in this classroom. There will be lead roles for a couple of people, and a number of bit parts."

As Jessica started out the door, Lila caught up with her. "Did you hear?" she asked, smiling sweetly. "There'll be bit parts, as well as the lead. I'm sure you'll get *some* kind of role, Jessica."

"Yes," Jessica said coolly. "I'm sure I'll get the *lead* role. And I hope you'll enjoy your *bit* part, Lila."

Lila scowled and marched off, while Jessica went to her locker to get her social studies book. *One of us is going to be very disappointed*, Jessica told herself grimly as she walked down the hall. *And it's not going to be me!*

"Hey, Leslie," Elizabeth said, catching up with her on their way to social studies. "What jobs did you choose?"

Leslie hesitated. While she was filling out her form, she had heard two voices inside her head—Deirdre's voice telling her to audition, and another voice, her own, telling her not to audition. But Deirdre's voice had been louder. Leslie had finally written actress on the first line, scriptwriter on the second, and costume designer on the third. But

the minute she turned in the form, she had regret-
ted her decision.

"I put down scriptwriter and costume
designer," she said. "And actress." Leslie figured
there was no point in telling Elizabeth that actress
had been her first choice. "What did you put
down?"

"Scriptwriter was my first choice, too," Elizabeth said. "Maybe we'll be working together."

"That would be great," Leslie said as enthusiastically as she could. "I think the scriptwriters
are the backbone of every movie. Without a good
script, a movie is nothing."

"Absolutely," Elizabeth agreed as they walked
down the hall. "Scriptwriting is definitely the most
important job."

Leslie nodded, but no matter what she said,
she still thought that good acting was really the
most important part of a movie. *Oh, well*, she con-
soled herself, *I'll probably enjoy scriptwriting. Anyway, acting isn't for me. How could I ever be a real
actress when I'm so scared, I can't even tell my friends
the truth?*

Three

◆

Elizabeth was sitting on the floor in the upstairs hall that evening, talking with Amy on the telephone.

"Maybe the story could involve a vampire who falls in love with a human girl," Elizabeth suggested.

"A vampire is pretty good," Amy said. "Or how about if a boy buys something, like a robot toy, and it turns out to be an alien?"

"Where's the love story?" Elizabeth asked. "We *have* to have a love story."

"Well, maybe this kid has a girlfriend, and the alien falls in love with her." She laughed. "You know, a real romantic triangle—boy, girl, and alien."

"That's cute," Elizabeth agreed. "But maybe

instead of buying a toy, the boy plants something that grows into an alien."

"That's good!" Amy cried. "But maybe instead of growing an *alien*, he could grow *The Slime*!"

Elizabeth laughed. "What's The Slime?"

"You know," Amy said. "It's green smelly stuff, really gross, that oozes all over the place, swallowing everything in its path. The Slime that ate Sweet Valley!"

"Oh, *that* Slime," Elizabeth said, laughing. "Amy, that's an absolutely fabulous title. *The Slime That Ate Sweet Valley*."

"Do you really think so?" Amy asked.

"I really think so," Elizabeth replied. "Mr. Bowman will love it. The guys will think it's terrific. And Lila and the Unicorns will hate it!"

"I know!" Amy laughed. "Can't you just imagine? Whoever gets the girl's lead will be kissed on the mouth by a hunk of smelly green slime!"

At that moment, Jessica came running up the stairs. "Elizabeth, aren't you off the phone *yet*?" she asked. "Hurry up! I've got something important I want to tell you."

"I'm almost finished, Jess," Elizabeth said. "Amy and I were trying to come up with a title for the movie, and Amy had a great idea."

"What is it?" Jessica asked.

"Are you *sure* you want to hear Amy's idea?" Elizabeth asked Jessica.

"Of course," Jessica insisted.

"It's *The Slime That Ate Sweet Valley.*"

"*The Slime That Ate Sweet Valley!*" Steven said as he came down the hall. "Hey, Lizzie, that's a cool title."

"No, it's *not* a cool title!" Jessica cried. "It's totally gross! How can a serious actress even *think* of starring in a film with such a yucky title?"

"I heard that!" Amy said on the phone. "That settles it, Elizabeth. We're going to call our film *The Slime That Ate Sweet Valley.* But don't tell Jessica that the star has to *kiss* The Slime. If that got out, I'll bet *no* one would audition for the part!"

"You're right! I'll see you tomorrow, Amy." Elizabeth hung up and turned to Jessica. "So, what's this important thing you've got to tell me?"

"Forget my news for a minute. What's the idea of scaring me with a stupid title like *The Slime That Ate Sweet Valley?*" Jessica demanded.

"C'mon, Jess. Tell me," Elizabeth urged.

"Oh, all right. Actually, it's news for Steven, too," Jessica said.

"What's for me, too?" Steven asked.

Jessica lowered her voice. "I just heard Mom and Dad talking about the trip they're planning to Mexico."

"I'm glad they're going on vacation," Steven said. "I just hope they don't get some drippy sitter to take care of us."

"That's the point!" Jessica whispered loudly. "I think they really *are* considering leaving us by ourselves. I heard them talking about how mature we are and how much they trust us."

"I don't know," Elizabeth said doubtfully. "I'm not sure I'm ready to be *that* responsible."

Steven shook his head. "*You* may not be, Lizzie, but *I* am. What would the guys at school think if they knew that somebody was *baby*-sitting me? No way!"

"Steven's right," Jessica said grimly. "Listen, you guys, we've got to act really grown-up for the next couple of weeks. We want Mom and Dad to think we can take care of ourselves."

"Yeah," Steven said. "So grow up, you two."

Jessica flipped her hair. "Don't tell *me* to grow up, Steven. I'm *already* mature enough to have a starring role in a movie! In just a few weeks, I'll be famous!"

Elizabeth grinned. She wondered what Jessica would say if she knew that the price of fame was a kiss from The Slime!

On Thursday morning, Mr. Bowman brought the school's video camera to class.

"A video camera is often called a camcorder,"

he explained. "All you have to do is hold it up and look through the viewfinder. Then you push this button and shoot. The camcorder automatically focuses and changes the exposure to match the available light. Best of all, its captures sound."

"Hey, a sound camera!" Aaron exclaimed. "That's terrific!"

Mr. Bowman nodded. "Unfortunately, this camera is pretty old, and the sound isn't very sharp. And it doesn't work well in low-light situations. Do any of your parents have a newer model we could borrow?"

Jessica raised her hand. "We have a camcorder," she said. "It's only a year or two old. I'm sure we could borrow it."

"Actually," Lila said loudly, "my father is planning to buy one this week. A brand-*new* one," she added smugly. "I'm sure the sound will be *very* sharp. And it'll probably take pictures in the dark."

Jessica sat back in her seat and crossed her arms over her chest. Lila was her best friend, but sometimes she was so snotty, even a best friend couldn't stand her!

"Tell you what," Mr. Bowman said. "If it's all right with the Wakefields and Mr. Fowler, we'll borrow *both* camcorders. Several cameras mean we'll need several camera people." Mr. Bowman put down the video camera and walked over to the VCR. "Let's take a look at the horror film I've brought, paying special attention to the camera techniques."

Mr. Bowman turned off the lights, and for the next half-hour the class watched part of a classic version of *Dr. Jekyll and Mr. Hyde*. But what was even spookier than the movie was the fact that the VCR kept turning itself off and then on again, even though nobody went anywhere near the controls.

The first two times it happened, Mr. Bowman just shook his head. The third time, he went up to the set and tested its controls. "The ghost of the English classroom strikes again," he said. "The snake, the cricket, the easel, and now the VCR. It looks like our classroom is haunted."

Jessica watched Pete closely. She knew he was responsible. He had his hand in his pocket when the VCR went off the fourth time, but she could not figure out how he was doing it—or why. Finally, Pete caught her looking at him. He winked at her mischievously and pulled his hand out of his pocket. The VCR did not turn itself off again.

After they had watched the tape for a while, Mr. Bowman stopped the VCR and they talked about what exactly made the movie spooky. Then they talked about how they could turn spooky elements into something funny in *their* film.

"Sometimes it's easiest to start off with a

title," Mr. Bowman said. "Has anybody come up with any ideas?"

"How about *Dr. Hekyll and Mr. Jyde*?" Winston suggested.

"That's good, Winston," Mr. Bowman said over a ripple of laughter.

Elizabeth raised her hand. "Amy had a great idea," she said. "She thinks we should call the movie *The Slime That Ate Sweet Valley*."

"Hey, terrific!" Charlie called out, and the rest of the boys clapped. The Unicorns, however, were not pleased at all.

"That's a *terrible* title, Amy," Lila scolded. "It's dumb."

"It's worse than dumb," Ellen said scornfully. "It's stupid. I've never heard such a stupid title."

"I know," Amy said with a smile. "It's dumb and stupid. That's what makes it so perfect. And wait until you hear our idea for a plot!"

"After that gross title, I'm afraid to ask about the rest of it," Jessica moaned.

"Come on, Amy," Randy urged. "Tell us."

"It's about a kid who grows plants in his basement," Amy said. "Like cucumbers or something."

Elizabeth nodded. "Right, giant cucumbers. He's growing them under grow lights."

"And one day he goes down to the basement," Amy went on, "and his prize cucumber has turned into . . . The Slime!"

"What does The Slime look like?" Jerry asked.

"It's green and bubbly, of course," Winston said, "and smelly and oozy. Your typical moderately aggressive slime mold."

"A five-hundred-pound rotten green cucumber!" Charlie said, and the class roared.

"And this five-hundred-pound rotten green cucumber eats everything in its path," Winston said gleefully.

"It eats the guy's older sister," Leslie put in. "His *nagging* older sister who's always telling him to clean up the basement."

"And maybe his grandmother," Sophia suggested excitedly. "His grandmother wants to make pickles out of the boy's cucumbers, and when she comes to pick them, The Slime gets her."

"And his girlfriend!" Amy looked at Lila. "Remember, this is a love story, too. The Slime has to fall in love with the guy's girlfriend."

"Yeah, but the guy's got to rescue his girlfriend," Aaron said excitedly.

"More victims," Charlie said, rubbing his hands together. "The Slime needs more victims."

"A teacher," Elizabeth suggested mischievously. "Maybe one of The Slime's victims could be an English teacher."

"English teachers! Yummy!" Winston called out.

Mr. Bowman laughed. "How about an English

teacher and a principal?" he suggested. "Maybe Mr. Clark would agree to be in our movie."

"Would he have to audition?" somebody asked, and the class erupted into laughter again.

Mr. Bowman held up his hand for quiet. "I can see that you guys are really getting into the spirit of things," he said. "But the bell's about to ring—"

"Already?" Charlie asked. "You mean, the whole period's gone? But we just got started."

"Time flies when you're having fun, Charlie," Mr. Bowman remarked. "Don't forget the auditions this afternoon, here in this classroom. From the sound of things, we're going to need three main characters—a boy, a girl, and—"

"The Slime!" the class shouted.

Mr. Bowman nodded. "I'll have an audition script prepared for those who want to try out for the three lead roles. And it looks as if we're going to need quite a few bit players. So far, we've got a sister and a grandmother, and I'm sure the scriptwriters—when they're chosen—will be able to come up with several other victims. Anybody who wants to volunteer to be eaten by The Slime, please come and audition this afternoon."

"How do you audition for the part of a Slime victim?" Caroline asked.

"Just be yourself, Caroline," Mr. Bowman said as the bell rang.

"If you ask me," Lila said to Amy, Elizabeth, and Leslie as they were leaving the classroom, "the whole idea is just plain stupid. What kind of a love story is this anyway?"

"A funny love story," Elizabeth replied.

"A *ridiculous* love story," Jessica added pointedly. "I mean, a silly part like this could be totally disastrous for your acting career, Lila."

"Yes, it could also be disastrous for *your* career, couldn't it, *Jessica*?" Lila replied. "Maybe you should reconsider your decision to try out for a lead role. I know you wouldn't want to star in a *ridiculous* movie with a *stupid* title. Your career would be over before it even began."

With a laugh, Elizabeth, Amy, and Leslie left Jessica and Lila, each trying desperately to convince the other to drop out of the auditions.

"This has got to be the funniest thing that's happened in Sweet Valley since—I don't remember when!" Amy said.

"Are you going to try out for a part as a Slime victim, Amy?" Elizabeth asked.

"Maybe," Amy said. "How about you, Leslie? You're going to audition, aren't you?"

Leslie swallowed hard. "I don't think so."

"But didn't you put down actress on your form?" Elizabeth asked.

"Yes," Leslie admitted. "But, well, the truth is that I—well, I'm scared to audition."

"But it's just the kids from the sixth grade!" Amy protested. "There's nothing to be scared about."

Leslie bit her lip. "Maybe not for you, but there is for me. I just know I'd make a big mistake, and then everybody would laugh."

"But, Leslie," Elizabeth argued, "the actors in this movie will be *trying* to make people laugh."

"Well, maybe." Leslie fidgeted with the strap of her backpack and then took a step backward. "Listen, you guys, I'll see you later, OK?" As she hurried off, Leslie was sure that Elizabeth and Amy thought she was one of the biggest jerks around!

Four

◇

Mandy looked critically at Jessica as they made their way through the lunch line. "What's with you today? You look like a nervous wreck. Is it the auditions this afternoon?"

"Yes," Jessica admitted as she added a bowl of Jell-O and a bag of cookies to her already full tray. Being nervous always made her hungry.

"But I didn't think you wanted the role," Mandy said. "Didn't you tell Lila that a movie like *The Slime* would be bad for your reputation as a serious actress?"

Jessica nodded. "Of course that's what I told Lila. But I only said it because I thought I could get her to change her mind about auditioning."

"Well, you didn't," Mandy replied as they headed toward the cash register. "I heard her telling Ellen that she practiced all last night in front of the mirror. She's determined to get that part."

"I know. It's really too bad that she *won't* get it, though," Jessica said firmly.

"Seriously, Jess," Mandy pressed, "I'm sort of surprised that you really *do* want the female lead in *The Slime*."

Jessica paid for lunch and waited while Mandy paid for hers. "A good actress should be able to play a lot of different roles, not just serious ones," Jessica replied when Mandy joined her. "And lots of really good actresses got their start in comedy, you know."

"You don't have to convince me that comedy is important! Remember, I was the one who came up with our vaudeville number for the social studies contest!" Mandy smiled. "I'd be trying out for one of the bit parts if I weren't so busy with the Drama Club. I can't even watch you audition today because of practice. But I'll be rooting for you."

Jessica nodded. "Thanks, Mandy. It makes me feel good to know that my friends—some of them, anyway—are behind me."

When classes were over that afternoon, Jessica hurried to Mr. Bowman's room. When she got there, there was a note on the door saying that the auditions had been moved to the auditorium. Jessica charged off to the auditorium and joined Lila and Ellen.

"Why did Mr. Bowman move the auditions?" Jessica asked as she sat down in the darkened second row. The stage lights were up, and the stage itself was brightly lit.

"Because so many people decided to try out," Lila replied. "Wait a minute—I thought *you* decided that the movie was so stupid, you didn't want to be in it?"

Jessica shrugged. "No," she said. "I thought *you'd* decided that."

"Wishful thinking, Jess," Lila said. "I think it's a *challenge* to play a comic role. A good actress has to be versatile."

The first few rows of the darkened auditorium were beginning to fill up. Jessica saw that Brooke, Caroline, Winston, Tom McKay, and Randy were there. Elizabeth and Amy came in with Sophia and sat at the end of the first row. Before long, almost the entire sixth grade was there.

"I'm glad Tom is trying out," Jessica whispered to Lila. "He's *very* cute. He'd be perfect as the male lead." Jessica could imagine Tom wrapping his arms around her and giving her a long, romantic kiss. She smiled secretly. Of course, it would make Aaron jealous, but that was just too bad. Actresses' boyfriends had to learn to make sacrifices.

"Yes, Tom would be *my* first choice," Lila said significantly. "Of course, Ken Matthews is also very cute, but he's shorter than me, which might look a little silly if we have to kiss."

"Ken and *I* are the same height," Jessica remarked. "We'd look fabulous together."

"But it would be absolutely *disastrous* if either Winston or Randy got the lead," Lila added, ignoring Jessica's last remark. "I wouldn't want the part if it meant I had to play opposite either of *them*."

"Yeah," Ellen agreed. "Winston is a jerk, even if he is a Booster."

"And Randy is a total nerd," Jessica added.

"I don't think either of you has anything to worry about," Ellen said confidently. "Neither of them will get the part. Winston's too much of a clown, and Randy's too shy."

Just then, Mr. Bowman came to the edge of the stage. "OK, gang," he said, "we'll begin by auditioning the people who want to try out for a lead role. After that, we'll audition anybody who wants a role as a victim." Mr. Bowman held up some papers. "Candidates for the lead roles, this is your script. It's a short dialogue between a boy and a girl. As you'll see when you read it, the two are having an argument, though they make up in the end. There's plenty of emotion in the piece, and some comedy, too, so it will give you a chance to show your acting stuff."

Winston raised his hand. "We're trying out now for the part of The Slime, too—right?"

"Right," Mr. Bowman said. "And don't assume that The Slime has to be a boy. In the right costume, a girl can be *just* as slimy as a boy."

"Of course, Jessica," Lila whispered, "if you don't get the lead role, you can always play The Slime."

"What's wrong with *you* playing The Slime?" Jessica snapped.

"I'll make the announcement of the three lead roles in class tomorrow morning," Mr. Bowman continued, "as well as some of the minor roles." He came down from the stage and began to hand out audition scripts. "Of course," he added, "we won't know exactly how many bit players we need until our scriptwriters tell us how many victims The Slime is going to consume. Some of you may not know for a few more days whether or not you're going to be devoured."

Jessica reached eagerly for the script Mr. Bowman handed her and scanned it quickly. It was exactly the kind of dialogue she liked.

"OK," Mr. Bowman said, "let's get started." He climbed onto a stool at the corner of the brightly lit stage and looked down at a list of names in his hand. "Lila, you and Winston can be first."

Lila groaned, and Jessica smothered a giggle.

"Break a leg," she whispered as Lila reluctantly got to her feet.

Lila stomped up onto the stage and snatched the script from Mr. Bowman. Without waiting for Winston, she began to read quickly.

" 'I've told you over and over, Amanda,' " she read, " 'but you never hear me. Why don't you just shut up and listen for a change? The truth is that—' "

"Hey, wait," Winston objected. "*You're* Amanda, Lila. I'm Bob. I'm supposed to be saying all that stuff."

"I know what I'm doing," Lila snapped. "These are *my* lines. Can't you read the cue? It says—"

"The cue says they're *my* lines," Winston said. "Let's start over again."

One of the boys in the audience snickered. "Way to go, Lila!" he called out.

Winston cleared his throat and read the lines Lila had just performed. When he came to a stop, there was a silence.

"What's the matter, Lila?" he asked. "Are you lost?"

"I'm not lost! I just can't find my place!"

"We're right here," Winston said as he pointed to her lines. Lila began to read, her tone as flat as cardboard.

"Hang on, Lila," Mr. Bowman said. "Remember, this is supposed to be an *argument*. Loosen up. Yell a little."

Jessica covered her mouth with her hand to hide her grin. *Poor Lila!* she thought. *Even her yells are boring!* When it was over, Lila marched off the stage and back to her seat, red-faced and humiliated. Jessica could not help but feel sorry for her, but she breathed a little easier. With Lila out of the way, the lead was definitely hers!

Mr. Bowman called out Brooke's name and teamed her up with Tom. Jessica folded her arms across her chest and frowned. This was an unforeseen development! Brooke's father was a scriptwriter so Brooke probably knew a lot about acting. Jessica watched Brooke and Tom play the scene. They were far better than Lila and Winston, and Jessica's nervousness came back in full force.

"Jessica, it's your turn," Mr. Bowman announced when Brooke and Tom had left the stage. "And, Randy, you play the boy this time. OK?"

Jessica's heart sank. "Randy Mason!" Lila said with a giggle. "The biggest nerd in Sweet Valley! Good luck, Jessica. I'm sure the two of you were made for each other."

"Oh, shut up, Lila," Jessica hissed as she stood up and headed toward the stage. *What a disaster*, she thought.

"Hi, Jessica," Randy said shyly. "I hope you're not as scared as I am."

"What makes you think I'm scared?" Jessica asked. *This is just great,* she thought. *Not only do I have to audition with a nerd, I have to audition with a* scared *nerd!*

"OK, you two," Mr. Bowman said. "Let's get started."

" 'I've told you over and over again, Amanda,' " Randy said firmly, " 'but you never hear me. Why don't you just shut up and listen for a change? The truth is that—' "

Randy's voice was firm and confident, and it projected all the way to the back of the auditorium. For a moment Jessica was so surprised that she almost missed her cue.

" 'Now, it's *your* turn to listen to *me,*" Jessica read. " 'The truth is that *you're* a pain, Bob. A total pain!' "

" 'You think so?' " Randy laughed sarcastically. " 'Since when are you an authority on who's a pain, Amanda?' "

By the middle of their argument, Jessica found herself yelling at Randy furiously. His performance as Bob was so convincing that she forgot he was only acting! And when it came time to make up, Randy delivered Bob's apologies with so much genuine sweetness that Jessica almost wanted to cry.

When Jessica and Randy were finished, there was a split second of silence. Then everyone in the darkened auditorium began to clap and whistle. Without a doubt, she and Randy had turned in the best performance of the afternoon.

"That was a fine performance," Mr. Bowman said. "Jessica, your crying at the end was perfect. And Randy, I had no idea you were such a good actor."

"It's one of my deep, dark secrets," Randy said with a shy laugh. And then, as he followed Jessica off the stage, he tripped and almost went sprawling. Jessica rolled her eyes. *How did Randy ever learn to act*, she thought, *when he hasn't even learned to walk!*

Jessica took a seat in the front row next to Brooke. She was going to get the role—she *knew* it. She smiled over her shoulder at Lila, but Lila avoided meeting her eyes.

"You were great, Jessica," Brooke said. "And so was Randy. Who would ever have guessed that he was such a good actor!"

Jessica shrugged. "I don't think he's so great," she said. "I think he just happened to have a good day. Or that he did a good job because he was teamed up with me. After all, I've had a *lot* of experience."

"Maybe," Brooke said. "But whatever the reason, Randy gave a really strong performance."

Jessica shrugged and settled back to watch Caroline and Ken. Caroline was not very good at all, she thought, but Ken was OK. *If Tom doesn't get the leading role*, Jessica thought, *Ken will be a good second choice.*

When Caroline and Ken left the stage, Mr. Bowman looked down at his list. "OK," he said, "we have one more person to audition—Leslie Forsythe. Leslie, how about if you pair up with Randy? I'm sure he won't mind reading the script one more time."

Behind her, Jessica heard Lila laugh. "Leslie Forsythe?" Lila said. "What a joke! What makes her think she's an actress?"

Ellen giggled. "Yeah. I think Leslie should play The Slime. That's the perfect part for her."

"Leslie?" Mr. Bowman asked again, peering out into the darkened auditorium. "Are you out there?"

"I don't think she's here," Caroline answered. "Maybe she changed her mind and decided not to try out."

"Maybe she's just late," Elizabeth suggested.

"Well," Mr. Bowman replied, "if Leslie shows up before we're finished for the day she can still audition for the lead. OK," he continued, "everybody's who's here to try out for a bit part, up onstage. The rest of you can leave if you want."

*   *   *

Leslie waited until Mr. Bowman and those who wanted bit parts were busy onstage and all those who had already auditioned had left. Then she slipped out of her seat and made her way up the aisle. Out in the empty hall, she leaned against the door, blinking back the tears.

She really had *wanted* to try out. She had been thinking about the auditions all day, trying to work up her courage to get up onstage and face a real live audience. And she had almost succeeded. She had remembered Deirdre's encouragement and the support Amy and Elizabeth had given her, and she had really thought she could do it.

She had arrived at the auditions just as Lila was making such an embarrassing mess of her audition. As she watched, her stomach had gotten tighter and her mouth drier. Leslie had shoved her fists into the pockets of her jeans. *Suppose I get up on the stage and do as badly as Lila—or even worse! Suppose my dreams of an acting career are just that—ridiculous dreams?* Leslie had thought desperately.

Then, after she had watched Brooke and Jessica perform, Leslie had felt even more discouraged. Brooke was a natural, and it was easy to see that Jessica was really experienced. Of course, a big part of Jessica's success was due to Randy, who was one of the best amateur actors Leslie had ever seen. But Jessica was good, no doubt about it. *What made me think I could compete with somebody like Jessica Wakefield?* she had thought.

Still, she might have had the courage to answer when Mr. Bowman called her name if it had not been for the cruel conversation she had overheard between Lila and Ellen. It had hurt her so much that she had almost cried. And then what made her auditioning completely impossible was the fact that she had been paired to act with Randy Mason.

And that was what Leslie absolutely, positively could *not* bring herself to do. For her deepest, most hidden secret—a secret even deeper and more carefully hidden than the fact that she wanted to be an actress—was the fact that she liked Randy better than any other boy she had ever met. She had always thought he was awfully nice, even if he was pretty shy. But in addition to being nice and smart, Leslie thought Randy was cute, too. She loved the way his dark hair fell across his forehead, and she thought it was adorable the way he kept pushing his glasses up on his nose.

But while the other girls seemed to be able to laugh and flirt with the boys they liked, Leslie was different. The more she liked a boy, the quieter and more shy she felt around him, the faster her heart beat, and the more her tongue got twisted up when she tried to speak. And Leslie liked Randy a *lot*. She knew that if she had had to get up there onstage to act with him, she would not have been able to say one single word!

Five

◇

When she got home later that afternoon, Jessica was feeling so happy and confident that she went into the kitchen and made a salad for dinner without even being asked.

Mrs. Wakefield came into the kitchen as Jessica was putting the salad in the refrigerator. "Thanks, Jess," she said. "I appreciate the help."

"You're welcome. Guess what, Mom? Today was the audition for our movie. And I'm almost a hundred percent sure that I got the part!"

Mrs. Wakefield smiled. "That's wonderful, Jessica! We'll talk about it more at dinner. Right now I'm trying to finish up some work on a new design project. Would you mind peeling some potatoes and keeping an eye on the meat loaf?"

"Sure, Mom," Jessica answered. "I'm in such a good mood, I may even set the table!"

"I'll believe *that* when I see it!" Mrs. Wakefield laughed and headed back to the den, where she did most of the projects she brought home from the interior decorating firm where she worked part time.

Jessica was peeling the last of the potatoes when Elizabeth came into the kitchen.

"You gave a great performance at the audition this afternoon, Jess," Elizabeth said. "I think you're a sure thing for the part."

"Which part?" Steven asked as he strode into the kitchen and grabbed an apple from the bowl on the table. "Are you going to play The Slime That Ate Sweet Valley?"

Jessica stuck her tongue out at her brother. "For your information, I'm going to play the female lead."

"For sure?" Steven asked.

"Well, not for sure—yet," Jessica admitted. "But I *think* I'll get it. My audition was pretty fabulous."

"You were definitely better than Brooke, and a million times better than Lila," Elizabeth said.

"But what I want to know," Steven persisted, "is who's going to play The Slime. He's the most important character."

"Who says The Slime has to be a boy?" Elizabeth teased. "Maybe The Slime is a girl."

"Everyone knows The Slime is a guy," Steven explained patiently.

"I think Lila would make a good Slime," Jessica said.

"If Lila Fowler plays The Slime," Steven said on his way out, "you can bet I'll be there to watch."

When he had gone, Elizabeth turned to Jessica. "You know, the one who really surprised me today was Randy. I had no idea he was such a natural-born actor!"

Jessica shrugged and dropped the last potato into the pot.

"Maybe you weren't impressed with Randy's performance," Elizabeth said, "but everybody else was. I heard a lot of people say that he'd be perfect for the boy's lead."

"Well, they're wrong!" Jessica shouted. "Randy Mason only gave a good performance because of my acting experience. Or maybe he accidentally had a good day. But that doesn't change the fact that he's a first-class nerd. Did you see him stumble when he went offstage? And those ridiculous glasses! How will it look if the leading man has to keep pushing up his glasses?"

Elizabeth laughed. "Ridiculous glasses? I seem to remember that *you* recently wore glasses, Jess.

And I don't believe that Randy's great performance was just an accident—*or* all due to you."

"Of course it was," Jessica replied. "Randy is the shyest guy in school."

"But he's never been shy in front of an *audience*," Elizabeth pointed out. "He's an entirely different person when he's up in front of the sixth grade doing his presidential stuff."

"Lizzie, as far as I'm concerned, he's still the same old nerd," Jessica said, her earlier good mood now pretty much gone. "Listen, since I got dinner, I think it's only fair that you take my turn at the dishes tonight."

"You got dinner?" Elizabeth asked. "You mean, you peeled potatoes."

"I made a salad, too. A *big* salad."

Elizabeth grinned. "All right. I'll *help* with the dishes. How's that?"

"Oh, OK," Jessica grumbled. *Why did Elizabeth have to bring this up!* she thought as she headed upstairs to her room. *Now I have something new to worry about—a geeky leading man!*

Mr. Bowman called the class to order as soon as the bell had rung. "I'll start off by announcing the names of our three lead actors," he said. "For the female lead, I've chosen . . . Jessica Wakefield!"

As Elizabeth gave her sister the thumbs-up

sign, she noticed that everybody in the room was clapping except for Lila.

Mr. Bowman let the applause die down. "Congratulations, Jessica," he said. "Now, the male lead will be . . . Randy Mason."

There was more clapping, and several of the boys called out, "Way to go, Randy!" Elizabeth looked back at Jessica and saw that this time Jessica was the only one who was not clapping. Lila was pounding her hands together with wicked glee.

"There's one more major role to fill," Mr. Bowman continued, "and that's the role of The Slime. There are two people, either of whom, in my opinion, could play a first-rate Slime. It's really a tie between them. But I've decided to offer the role to . . . Lila Fowler!"

"Me," Lila squawked. "*Me*—play The Slime! You must be joking!"

Elizabeth suppressed a giggle, but the rest of the class, including Jessica, laughed loudly.

"I was afraid a girl might not want the role," Mr. Bowman said. "But in my view, it's a far more challenging role than either the boy or the girl lead. The Slime has so much *character*. Are you sure I can't convince you to give it a try, Lila?"

"*Positive!*" Lila shouted.

"OK, then," Mr. Bowman said. "The other

person I had in mind for the role is . . . Winston Egbert. How about it, Winston? Will you play The Slime?"

"I'd love to," Winston said promptly. "It's the role of my dreams!"

Mr. Bowman laughed. "Well, I'm glad to hear that. I'm sure you'll turn in a fine performance. Now, in addition to the three main roles, I've got two bit parts to announce today. As I said before, there'll be more parts later as the scriptwriters round out the plot. Brooke Dennis will play the part of the boy's older sister, and Caroline Pearce will be his grandmother. And Mr. Clark, our very own principal, has agreed to play the role of—you guessed it—the principal."

Winston rubbed his hands together eagerly. "You mean, I get to eat a *principal*? Yum, yum," Winston said. "I can't wait."

"Now that the major roles are settled," Mr. Bowman said, "I'll make the other job assignments. Maybe you'd better copy down the names."

Elizabeth took out a piece of paper and started copying what Mr. Bowman wrote on the blackboard. At the top of the list he put his own name as director. Colin Harmon was the director's assistant. Under scriptwriter he wrote Elizabeth's name as well as Amy's, Leslie's, and Maria's. Peter DeHaven was chief camera person, and Jerry was a camera operator. Charlie and Todd were set designers and Mandy was a set carpenter. Aaron was responsible for music. Pete was in charge of special effects and film editing. Lois Waller was costume manager and seamstress. Tom was locations manager, and Ellen was his helper. Lila was in charge of the clean-up crew, and several other students were on the crew itself.

"Clean-up?" Lila asked indignantly when she saw Mr. Bowman writing her name. "Why do I have to be responsible for clean-up?"

"Everybody has to do their share, Lila," Mr. Bowman said reasonably, "and clean-up is especially important. No matter where we're filming, the set has to be cleaned up after we're finished shooting for the day."

"Well, I think you'll need to find somebody else," Lila said huffily. "*I'm* going to run a camcorder."

"Hey, wait," Pete objected. "We've only got two camcorders, Lila—the one that belongs to the school, and the one we're borrowing from the Wakefields. And we've already got two people assigned to camerawork."

Lila raised her chin. "We've got *three* camcorders," she said. "My father bought a brand-new one yesterday, and he paid a fortune for it. It has stereo sound and requires very low light levels—*and* it weighs less than two pounds. I think it should be our *main* camera."

"If it's one of the really expensive models," Mr. Bowman said, "your father might not want to loan it to us. We can't guarantee that it won't be damaged."

"He'll loan it, all right," Lila said determinedly, "but on one condition."

Elizabeth smiled. She was pretty sure she knew what that one condition would be.

"What's that?" Mr. Bowman asked.

"That *I'm* the only one who operates it," Lila replied. "I'll be so busy operating the camcorder that I won't have time for clean-up."

Elizabeth rolled her eyes. She had been right. If Lila couldn't be the star in front of the camera, she would be the star *behind* it.

"OK," Mr. Bowman said, as he turned back to the board and wrote Lila's name under camera operator. "I'll make Ken Matthews chief of the clean-up crew. But I'm putting your name on the clean-up list." Mr. Bowman turned around and smiled. "You never know, Lila. You may discover you're quite a hit with the dust mop!"

Leslie was glad that the bell had rung. For most of the class, she had been fighting tears. She was really happy that Randy had gotten the boy's lead, and she was glad—sort of—that Jessica had gotten the girl's lead.

Leslie sighed. Jessica would do a good job,

especially with Randy's help. Still, she could not help but imagine how it would have been if *she* had gotten the girl's part. But it was too late now. Jessica had gotten the part, and there was absolutely nothing that she could do about it.

Leslie was gathering her books when Elizabeth stopped by her desk. "I'm so glad to be a scriptwriter," she said. "Aren't you, Leslie?"

Leslie swallowed and smiled weakly. "Yes," she said. "And I'm glad we're working together, Elizabeth."

Amy joined Leslie and Elizabeth as they walked toward the door. "Hey, Leslie, what happened to you yesterday? I thought you were going to audition for a part."

"Yeah," Elizabeth pressed.

Leslie cleared her throat. She knew it would be best to tell Elizabeth and Amy the truth—that she had chickened out. But if she told them *that* much, she would probably also have to tell them that she had heard what Lila and Ellen had said at the auditions. Then she would probably have to tell them how she felt about Randy. And there was no way she was going to tell *anyone* about that special secret.

"I, uh, had something really important to do," she said uncomfortably. "I'm not really crazy about acting, anyway. I wrote actress because I couldn't think of anything else to write." Leslie laughed nervously and pulled her books close against her. "Hey, excuse me, will you?" she said quickly. "I just remembered something I have to get out of my locker."

"I get this really funny feeling that something's wrong with Leslie," Amy said when Leslie had hurried off.

"I get the same feeling," Elizabeth said as they started to walk down the hall again. "In fact, I thought she looked as if she was trying hard not to cry."

Amy frowned. "I wonder what it is? Did we say something wrong? The trouble is that we don't know Leslie very well. I mean, she's usually so *quiet*. The only time she's ever opened up was the other day when we went to Sweet Valley Video."

"You're right," Elizabeth replied. "Movies seem to be her passion."

"I think we should get to know her better," Amy said firmly. "Maybe she won't be so shy when she feels more comfortable with us. I think I'll walk home with her after school today."

"You're definitely going to have a better time this afternoon walking home with Leslie than Jessica and I are going to have at the dentist!" Elizabeth groaned.

"You can be sure of that!" Amy replied. "I'll

see what I can find out and call you tonight. Leslie Forsythe has a mystery, and I intend to know what it is!''

Jessica was standing in the lunch line that Friday when Janet Howell joined her. Janet, who was Lila's cousin, was an eighth grader and the president of the Unicorns.

"Jessica," Janet said importantly, "I heard that you got the starring role in the sixth-grade movie. Congratulations! I'm sure you'll turn in a performance that will make the Unicorns proud."

"Thank you, Janet," Jessica said. "I'll do my very best."

"There *is* one small thing, though," Janet continued. "That title—*The Slime That Ate Sweet Valley*. I know it's meant to be funny, but it's . . . well, gross. I'm not sure that a movie with a title like that will be a credit to the Unicorns. I heard that Elizabeth is one of the scriptwriters. I think you should ask her to change the title."

"I don't think she will," Jessica said regretfully. "Everyone—except the Unicorns, of course—seems to like the title. And Mr. Bowman thinks it's really funny."

"Mr. Bowman!" Lila said huffily, coming up to them holding her lunch tray. "If you ask me, he's got a pretty weird sense of humor. Did you know, Janet, that he had the *nerve* to suggest that *I* should play The Slime?"

"He *didn't!*"

"He did!" Lila said indignantly. "It was an outrageous insult—not only to me, but to the Unicorns!"

"What did you say to him?" Janet asked.

"I told him he could find somebody else," Lila replied. "Furthermore, I told him that I intended to be a camera person. Wait until you see the neat camcorder my father bought, Janet. It's utterly fabulous, and it's so much fun to operate. And you know," she added authoritatively, "it's really the camerawork that makes or breaks a movie."

"Wait a minute, Lila," Jessica objected. "It's the *actors* who make or break a movie."

"Don't be naive, Jessica," Lila said. "Every sophisticated movie-goer knows that the actors are only puppets for the director to move around. The really *important* element is the camera. Without a good camera and an expert camera person, a film is a total flop."

"Lila," Jessica said hotly, "that is the stupidest idea I have ever heard. The actors are a hundred percent more important than the camera person. That's why actors get paid so—"

"Janet," Lila interrupted. "I've invited a few

special friends to come over this afternoon and try out my new camcorder. We're going to shoot as much video film as we want. Dad bought a whole *case* of it when he bought the camera. I'll have food, too, and I've got Dynamo's brand-new tape—the one *everybody's* been dying to hear."

"Terrific!" Janet said.

"I'd invite you, Jessica," Lila said, smiling sweetly, "but I know you've got a dentist appointment this afternoon. It's too bad you're going to miss such a *fabulous* party. I'm even inviting a few boys—like Aaron, for instance."

Jessica gritted her teeth. She had a sneaking suspicion that Lila was holding the party this afternoon just *because* she could not be there.

Jessica shrugged. "No big deal. I hope you have a good time at your little party."

"Oh, I will," Lila replied. "But the whole time, I'll be thinking of *poor* you, stuck in that horrible old dentist's chair! I hope he doesn't tell you that you have to have braces, Jessica. After all that time wearing those glasses, braces would be simply *too* humiliating!"

Six

◇

"The camera person is *far* more important than any other person in the movie," Lila announced as she, Jessica, Ellen, and Mandy walked into the dressing rooms at Valley Fashions on Saturday. "The camera angle makes or breaks an actress."

"Don't be ridiculous, Lila," Jessica said crossly as she tried on a green blouse. "We had this discussion yesterday. No camera person is more important than the actress!"

"That's how much *you* know," Lila answered smugly. "Everybody has a good side and a bad side. If the camera person wants to, she can focus on the bad side and make the actress look awful. *That's* why the camera person is so important."

"Better not turn your bad side to Lila," Mandy advised Jessica. "She might immortalize it."

"Smile," Lila called as she aimed her camera at Ellen, who was trying to wriggle out of a red sweater she had tried on over her blouse.

"I can't smile," Ellen said in a muffled voice. "My barrette is caught. Jessica, help me."

"Really, Ellen, you look *so* funny with your hair all messed up that way," Lila said, peering at Ellen through the viewfinder on the camcorder.

"Turn that thing off, Lila," Ellen said crossly, holding the sweater up in front of her face. "I look awful. My hair's a wreck, and my lipstick's all smeared, and—"

"I'm not going to turn it off," Lila said. "I need the practice. I want to be able to shoot like a pro by Monday. That doesn't give me much time."

"You should be a pro by now," Mandy said. "You took pictures all afternoon yesterday by the pool, you've taken pictures all morning—"

"And I'm going to *keep* taking pictures," Lila retorted, turning the camera on Jessica. "Practice makes perfect, you know. Jessica, you've missed a button on your blouse."

"Eek!" Jessica yelped and turned away from the camera. "Lila, what's *wrong* with you!"

"You're not going to show these pictures to anybody, are you?" Ellen asked nervously as she combed her hair.

"Don't worry about a thing," Lila assured

her, swiveling from Jessica back to Ellen. "We'll have a private screening so you can all see what you look like on videotape. But your secrets are safe with me."

When they left the boutique, Jessica suggested that they head for Casey's Ice Cream Parlor. "I'd like to see Lila take pictures and eat ice cream at the same time," she whispered to Mandy as the girls sat down in the booth. But no sooner had they ordered than Lila started shooting. She caught Jessica spilling a glass of water down her blouse and Mandy trying to lick maraschino cherry juice off the tip of her nose. Then Ellen's backpack fell on the floor, and Lila filmed her crawling around on her hands and knees, picking up lipstick and mascara and eye shadow.

"If I weren't so ticked off at Lila, I might think this was funny," Jessica said to Mandy.

"I've never seen Ellen so mad," Mandy said.

"I vote we leave," Jessica said when Ellen was back in her seat. "Either that, or we put a bag over Lila's camcorder."

"I vote we leave, too," Ellen said furiously. "I'm tired of having that stupid thing stuck in my face every two minutes."

Lila tossed her hair over her shoulders. "You're just jealous because *you* don't have the latest top-of-the-line camcorder."

When they were outside in the mall parking

lot, Lila spotted Aaron, Charlie, and Jerry riding their skateboards in a big concrete drainage ditch. "C'mon," Lila said. "Let's go get the guys on film!" Jessica groaned, but the boys were excited about showing off for the camera. They began to do stunts—jumps and power twists and power slides—as they roared down the drainage ditch. Lila's camcorder was still running when Aaron flipped a huge somersault while trying to do a turning slide.

"Aaron!" Jessica screamed. Aaron lay motionless at the bottom of the drainage ditch, a tangle of arms and legs. "Get an ambulance! Get a doctor, somebody!"

"Hey, Aaron," Charlie yelled. "You all right?"

"That was great, Aaron!" Lila called excitedly as she knelt down at the edge of the drainage ditch. "What a wipe-out! Listen, you've got to do it again! Only this time, somersault the other way, toward me. I didn't get a good shot of your face."

"You gotta be kidding, Lila." Aaron groaned and rolled over on his back. "I'm dying, and you want me to do it *again*?"

"Aaron, are you all right?" Jessica cried frantically as she scrambled down into the drainage ditch. "Are you hurt? Is anything broken? Should we call an ambulance?"

"That's good, Jessica," Lila called approvingly, and Jessica looked up to see her running the camcorder again. "Now, put your arms around Aaron and give him a big smoochy kiss while I zoom in closer."

Jessica knelt down beside Aaron and put an arm around him in an effort to help him get up.

"Don't get up, Aaron," Lila instructed. "Lie down on the ground and act like you're really hurt. You know—groan a lot. Come on, you guys, play it up! This is going to be a terrific scene."

Aaron finally managed to push Jessica away. "You're crazy, Lila," he said angrily as he pulled his helmet off. "Turn that stupid thing off before I turn it off for you!"

Lila turned off the camcorder. "I don't see why you're so mad," she protested. "We all could have won an Academy Award if there'd been a little more blood."

"There'll be blood next time," Aaron growled. *"Yours!"* He picked up his board and stalked away, Charlie and Jerry following him.

"I don't see why he's so mad," Lila muttered.

"Maybe it's because he didn't want his wipe-out on film for everyone to see," Mandy suggested. "Guys are funny that way."

"Yeah," Ellen agreed. "Or maybe your telling Jessica to kiss him in front of Charlie and Jerry was too embarrassing."

Jessica followed Mandy, Lila, and Ellen out of the parking lot. "If you can't figure out why people hate a camera recording their every move, it's because you've got the sensitivity of a *flea!*" she told Lila.

Mandy nodded. "You said it."

Leslie had been nervous about inviting Elizabeth, Amy, and Maria to her house for a scriptwriting brainstorm session. *What will we talk about all afternoon?* she wondered. When the girls arrived, Leslie took them to her room.

"Wow!" Amy said, looking around at the stacks of movie magazines, the autographed T-shirts hanging on the closet doors, and the posters and photos that covered every wall. "Look at all this stuff!"

"Hey, Maria," Elizabeth said. "There's a picture of you in your Softee Toilet Paper costume."

Maria laughed. "Leslie, you must have a poster for every movie made in the last five years!"

"And a lot from before *that*," Leslie replied proudly. "I've been collecting them since I was little. See that one over there? That's my prize possession. It was signed by Linda Larson—before she became a big star."

"Linda Larson," Amy said, "is one of my favorite actresses."

"I worked with her in *Star Bright*," Maria said.

"I know," Leslie replied quickly. "You were

great. Hey, did you know that Linda's little sister is getting into show business, too?"

"Really?" Maria asked.

"Yeah. I read it the other day in a movie trade magazine."

"Leslie, you know more about Hollywood than anyone I've ever met," Elizabeth said. "With the possible exception of Maria, of course."

"I *love* the movies," Leslie replied. "I mean, there's so much to *know* about the industry. The people, the films, the history—"

"Has anybody ever told you that you look like a different person when you talk about movies?" Amy asked suddenly.

"Really?" Leslie laughed self-consciously.

"It's like you're in love," Maria added wickedly.

Leslie laughed. "I *am* in love with the movies!"

"So why didn't you try out for the lead in *our* movie, Leslie?" Maria asked.

"We'd better get to work," Leslie said.

Elizabeth and Amy looked at each other and shrugged. "Yeah," Amy said. "Leslie's right. There won't *be* a movie if we don't *write* it."

"OK," Elizabeth said after they had been working for a while. "This is what we've got so far. Our hero is named Brian—that's Randy. He's got a girlfriend named Sherri—that's Jessica. For a science fair project, Brian is growing giant cucumbers in his basement."

"Under grow lights," Amy put in. "You can't grow cucumbers in the dark."

"Right. Under grow lights. Somehow, some Slime spores invade the cucumbers and begin to take them over. Does that sound right?"

"Sounds good so far," Maria said. "But we're going to need a basement in which to shoot."

"We could shoot in my basement," Leslie suggested. "It's unfinished. Besides, my mother's always after me to invite people over. Why not the entire cast and crew!"

"Can we take a look at it?" Amy asked.

"Sure. Let's go now." Leslie led them to the basement. "Well? What do you think?" she asked when they were gathered in the damp, dark room.

"This is perfect!" Elizabeth exclaimed. "It's really spooky."

Maria shivered. "Complete with spiders and cobwebs. The Slime will feel right at home attacking his victims."

"I'll tell Tom about this at school. And I'll bet Charlie and Todd will be glad they won't have to build a basement set," Amy said.

"But before we go any further," Elizabeth reminded them, "we have to figure out how Brian and Sherri finally get rid of The Slime."

"Why not have The Slime eat Brian and Sherri, too?" Maria suggested.

"I don't think Jessica would go for the idea of being eaten," Elizabeth said. "She'd say it was beneath her dignity as a leading lady."

"Anyway, I don't think we should end the movie with something terrible," Leslie protested. "Brian should be a hero and rescue Sherri—otherwise, where's the love story? I mean, there should be a big kiss at the end and romantic music and atmosphere."

"Amy told me about the love triangle." Maria grinned. "If The Slime falls in love with the heroine, *he* should have to kiss her, too!"

"That's great, Maria!" Amy said. "Sure—The Slime falls in love with Jessica—with Sherri, I mean. Then there's this really passionate scene where The Slime tells Sherri how much he loves her, and that he'll do anything for her. And then he kisses her."

"I can just imagine Jessica's face when she finds out she has to kiss The Slime! She'll be mad enough about having to kiss Randy," Maria said.

"Why?" Leslie asked quietly.

"Because the Unicorns think Randy's a nerd," Amy said.

"Randy's a nice guy," Maria protested.

"Yes," Leslie said quietly, "he is. Um—listen,

about The Slime—maybe, after he kisses Sherri, he could give up eating people."

"Why would he do that?" Amy asked.

"For love," Leslie explained. "He just sort of shrivels up and dies. And that's how the movie ends. A Beauty and the Beast type of plot."

"You mean Brian doesn't get to kill him?" Maria asked. "That's too bad. I thought of a great way to kill The Slime."

"Really?" Elizabeth asked. "How?"

"By sprinkling salt on him," Maria said triumphantly. "That's the way my mom kills those gross, slimy slugs that eat her lettuce. It'd be really dramatic on camera. Winston could writhe around a lot and yell, like he was poisoned."

"I like the nonviolent ending better—you know, The Slime dying for love," Leslie said.

"OK," Maria said. "But the guys may not be so thrilled!"

"We'll handle the guys," Elizabeth said. "But we need to come up with some more Slime victims. How about it, Leslie?"

"Who, me?" she asked lightly. "Forget it. I'm not an actress."

"But then why did you put down actress on your form?" Elizabeth asked.

Leslie laughed nervously. "I told you—I put down actress because I couldn't think of anything else. And, well—movies are sort of a hobby with me. Just because I love the movies doesn't mean I want to be an actress."

Elizabeth shrugged. "It's your choice."

The girls worked on the script for the rest of the afternoon. They agreed not to reveal any details about the script to anyone—except for Mr. Bowman, of course—until they were finished, which they hoped would be on Monday.

Late that afternoon, Elizabeth and Amy walked home together. "I can't wait until the script is finished and we start shooting," Elizabeth said.

"Yeah, the *script* is coming along great," Amy agreed. "But we didn't get any further toward solving Leslie's mystery."

"I know," Elizabeth agreed. "But I'll bet it has something to do with why she didn't audition for the movie!"

Seven

◇

By the time school was over on Monday, Jessica was fuming. "I'm fed up," she told Mandy, slamming her locker door so hard that it rattled. "I'm sick of Lila taking embarrassing pictures of me!"

"I saw her get you when the drinking fountain blew up in your face," Mandy said sympathetically.

"Yeah," Jessica replied grimly. "And when Kimberly Haver spilled chocolate milk all over my spaghetti at lunch. And in gym when I tried to spike the volleyball and ended up flat on my face. I wish Mr. Clark hadn't given her permission to practice during school!"

"I don't think she's *practicing*," Mandy replied. "I think she's filming because she *enjoys* catching people in embarrassing situations."

"Somebody should catch *her* in an embarrassing situation," Jessica muttered between clenched teeth. "I'll be glad when the scriptwriters are finished and we can start filming the movie. Maybe then she'll be so busy, she won't have time to bother us."

"I wouldn't bet on it!" Mandy replied.

Later that afternoon, Jessica was in her bedroom munching on potato chips and reading a fan magazine when she heard her twin coming up the stairs.

"Hey, Elizabeth," she called. "Is the script almost finished?"

"It's finished," Elizabeth said as she came in and sat down on Jessica's bed. The script was in her hand. "All but the finishing touches, anyway. It's good, too, and really funny."

Jessica held out her hand eagerly. "Can I read it?" she asked. "I can't *wait* to see what you've done with my part!"

"I don't know," Elizabeth said uncertainly. "We showed it to Mr. Bowman and he approved it, but the rest of the class won't see it until tomorrow."

"But why not let me see it tonight?" Jessica pleaded. "After all, I *am* the star. The star always gets to read the script *before* she even agrees to do the movie, not after."

Elizabeth hesitated for a moment. Then she

handed Jessica the script. "I guess it's OK," she said. "Rehearsals start tomorrow and run through Friday, so you might as well start learning your lines tonight."

"Terrific!" Jessica said enthusiastically. "When are we going to start videotaping?"

"Next Monday," Elizabeth replied. "Mr. Bowman said he thought we'd be through taping by Wednesday, so the film editors would have the rest of the week to work. He wants to show it to the school on the following Monday."

"That's only two weeks from today. Not much time," Jessica said excitedly. "I'd better get busy memorizing!"

"I'll set the table while you're reading," Elizabeth said as she stood up.

When Elizabeth left the room, Jessica settled back on her bed, reached for another handful of potato chips, and began to read. As she read, she started to giggle. Elizabeth was right. The script was really funny. She liked the character of Brian, even if she *didn't* like the boy who was playing him. She liked the way The Slime first started life as a large green cucumber, getting bigger and bigger until finally it emerged as a full-blown, mature Slime. She liked—

Jessica's eyes widened, and she sucked in her breath. She could hardly believe what she had just read. It couldn't be! The scriptwriters couldn't have written a scene like this! It was just too horrible for words!

"Elizabeth!" Jessica cried as she jumped off her bed, scattering potato chips onto the floor. She flew down the stairs with the script still clutched in her hand. "Elizabeth!" she shrieked. *"Elizabeth!"*

Elizabeth was in the kitchen when Jessica raced in. "This is awful!" Jessica cried frantically. "It's disgusting! It's repulsive! We can't have this in the movie!"

"Can't have what?" Elizabeth asked.

"We can't have *this*!" Jessica cried dramatically, pointing to the script. "This . . . this *kiss*!"

"Oh, you mean the part where The Slime falls in love with Sherri," Elizabeth said, trying to hide her smile. "Why? What's wrong with it?"

"You know very well what's wrong with it," Jessica retorted indignantly. "Kissing Winston Egbert—*that's* what's wrong with it!" She flung the script onto the table and crossed her arms over her chest. "There's no way I'm going to kiss that nerd," she said firmly.

"But you're not kissing Winston," Elizabeth pointed out reasonably. "You're kissing The Slime. He'll be all dressed up in a green Slime costume."

"But don't you see?" Jessica cried, stamping her foot. "It only makes it *worse* that Winston is The Slime. I'll look ridiculous! I'm *not* going to do it, and that's that. You'll just have to rewrite the scene."

"We can't rewrite it," Elizabeth said. "Mr. Bowman said it's one of the funniest scenes in the movie."

"Oh, no!" Jessica moaned. "I'm ruined! You mean, I really have to kiss Winston Egbert? On the *mouth*?"

Elizabeth nodded. "And I guess I should tell you about Mr. Bowman's other favorite scene. You probably haven't read that far yet," she said, still struggling not to laugh.

"I only read as far as kissing The Slime," Jessica replied. "That was far enough!"

"Well, Mr. Bowman's other favorite scene is at the end of the movie," Elizabeth explained. "The Slime dies, and Brian kisses Sherri." Jessica paled and recoiled a step. "It's really a very touching scene," Elizabeth added hurriedly.

"Brian kisses Sherri?" Jessica shrieked. "You mean, I've got to kiss Randy Mason, on top of Winston Egbert?"

"Not on top of Winston, exactly," Elizabeth said, this time not able to control her grin. "More like *beside* him. You see, The Slime dies and falls to the floor, and Brian puts his arms around Sherri, and—"

"You know what I mean!" Jessica cried hysterically. "I have to kiss Randy Mason, *too*?"

"Well, it is a love story," Elizabeth pointed out. "That's what you and the Unicorns wanted, wasn't it? You can't have a love story without a romantic scene at the end."

Jessica sat down at the table and put her face in her hands. "I have to kiss the two biggest nerds in the entire sixth grade! I'll be disgraced forever!"

"Winston and Randy are not nerds," Elizabeth protested. "Anyway, an actress—a really *professional* actress—does whatever the role demands. And it *is* supposed to be a *funny* movie, Jess."

"I'm ruined!" Jessica cried, ignoring Elizabeth. "Totally *ruined*! And it's all *your* fault."

"All my fault?" Elizabeth asked. "Wait a minute, Jess. I didn't—"

"Yes, you did," Jessica retorted. "It was *your* idea to make a spoof in the first place. *You* were in charge of the script. *You* could have left out the kissing scenes if you'd wanted to. But no, *you* thought it would be fun to see me totally humiliated in front of the entire school."

"C'mon, Jess," Elizabeth said. "You're a really good actress, and you'll be able to pull those scenes off beautifully no matter *how* you feel about Randy and Winston. Anyway, you know the old saying—'The show must go on.' "

Jessica sniffed loudly.

Elizabeth grinned and put her arm around Jessica. "C'mon, stop crying. I'll even help you with your lines. Then you'll really be ready for Winston and Randy when it's time to go in front of the camera."

"Oh," Jessica moaned. "I think I'm going to be sick!"

All Monday evening and well into the night, Jessica thought about *The Slime That Ate Sweet Valley*. And the more she thought about it, the more depressed and sorry for herself she felt. She had imagined that the starring role in the class movie would be a real triumph for her. But far from being a triumph, it was turning into a hideous nightmare. She was going to have to kiss Winston *and* Randy. And right in front of Lila and her camcorder, too! By lunchtime on Tuesday, everybody in Sweet Valley Middle School would know about her humiliation.

The next morning, Jessica felt so desperate that she found herself confessing to Mandy something she had never confessed to anyone except Elizabeth.

"It's not just the disgrace of kissing a couple of nerds," she said as she and Mandy walked to school that morning. "Or even the thought of doing it in front of Lila's camera."

"What is it then?" Mandy pressed.

Jessica could feel her face getting red. She trusted Mandy more than anyone else except her twin, but it was still hard to talk about something so embarrassing. "The truth is," she said slowly, "that I've never kissed anybody. Ever. Not even Aaron."

"But you're so cool around guys!" Mandy exclaimed. "I thought you had lots of experience!"

"Sure, I *act* cool because I *am* cool," Jessica said quickly. "But that doesn't mean I've had any kissing experience. I mean, I've seen plenty of kisses in movies and on TV, and Elizabeth told me what it's like when Todd kisses *her*. And once, this high school freshman kissed me, but I didn't kiss *him*. So those are all secondhand experiences—nothing like doing it yourself!"

"Well, if it makes you feel better, Jess, I've never kissed anyone, either," Mandy confided. "Everybody's got to start *somewhere*, you know."

"I know. But most people get to practice in *private*! And they get to do it over again if they don't get it right. But *I* have to do my first kiss—no, my first *two* kisses—in front of the camera! It's just not fair! I know I'll mess up, and my mistakes will be recorded forever!" Jessica sighed dramatically. "I'll be humiliated all over again whenever anyone sees the movie!"

"Well, if you're that upset," Mandy asked, "what are you going to do?"

"I don't know," Jessica moaned. "I thought about getting sick. Really deathly ill, I mean. Then

I'd have to go to the hospital, and everyone would feel sorry for me."

"That won't work," Mandy said authoritatively. She had spent some time in the hospital recently when she had had cancer. "To get into the hospital, you'd have to be sick for *real*, not just pretend-sick."

Jessica sighed. "Yeah. Unfortunately, I'm probably the healthiest person in the whole sixth grade."

"Maybe there's another out," Mandy said. "Maybe you could faint at rehearsal, right before you're supposed to kiss Winston. If you're all huddled up in a pitiful heap in the middle of the floor, Mr. Bowman *can't* make you go on with the scene!"

"I thought of that, too," Jessica said. "But remember, I've got to kiss Randy, too. I'd have to faint *twice*, and sooner or later somebody would figure out that I'm faking. Face it, I'm doomed. There's nothing to do but *do* it, no matter how awful it is."

When school was over for the day, all the kids involved with the movie were to report to the auditorium for the first run-through. In a last desperate effort, Jessica thought about not showing up at all and pretending the rehearsal had slipped her mind. But she knew Mr. Bowman would be very angry if she did that. *Well, if I have to go through with this*, she thought grimly on her way to the rehearsal, *at least I'm going to get some respect. I'm going to show everyone that I'm the star!*

"OK, everybody," Mr. Bowman said when they were all assembled. "Today the actors are going to read through their parts, while the crew gets familiar with the script. Tomorrow and the rest of the week, we'll continue reading and start blocking—that is, adding the action. We'll also bring in the cameras and start taping so we can get a feel for the way things look on film. Next Monday, we move to location in Leslie Forsythe's basement and start taping. Right now, let's have the three lead actors up here on the stage."

Jessica, Randy, and Winston pulled chairs into the center of the stage and sat down, while the bit players found seats in the front row, ready to come up onstage when it was their turn.

"OK, Randy," Mr. Bowman said as he sat down on a stool. "Let's take it from the top."

Randy opened his mouth to read his first line.

"Excuse me," Jessica interrupted, "but before we get started, I'd like some water. My throat is very dry."

Mr. Bowman turned to Colin. "Would you mind getting Jessica a glass of water, please, Colin?" he asked.

Randy cleared his throat and began to read again. When he had finished his opening lines,

Jessica began hers and then almost immediately paused to sip her water. After swallowing, she opened her mouth to start again, but suddenly she looked up and frowned.

"Could somebody please turn down the lights?" she asked. "They're very bright and they hurt my eyes."

"But it's so dark in here, I practically need a flashlight to see my script," Winston objected.

"I thought The Slime could see in the dark," Ken shouted from the front row.

"Pete," Mr. Bowman called out, "bring down the lights a little, please."

When the lights had dimmed, Jessica and Randy began again. They had run through two pages of dialogue when Jessica stopped again.

"What is it *this* time, Jessica?" Mr. Bowman asked with a touch of impatience.

"Maybe she wants the lights turned out altogether," Colin said sarcastically. "Then nobody will be able to see Beauty kiss The Slime."

"The lights are fine," Jessica said haughtily. "But I'm cold. Turn up the heat, please."

Caroline, who was waiting to read the part of Brian's grandmother, groaned. "The heat!" she exclaimed. "It's already roasting in here!"

"I think," Colin remarked, "Jessica's being a prima donna."

"Yeah," Charlie called from the wings. "She

thinks this is Hollywood and that she's got a multimillion-dollar contract."

Let them say whatever they want to say, Jessica told herself. *If I have to be mortified in front of the whole world by kissing the two biggest nerds in the entire sixth grade, I'm at least going to be treated like the star I am! And of course*, she thought, *the longer I delay the rehearsal, the less likely it is that we'll get to the kissing scenes today!*

Jessica's plan worked. The cast got only two-thirds of the way through the script before Mr. Bowman called it a day. And by the next afternoon, Jessica had come up with a plan designed to prevent her from rehearsing the kissing scenes for at least a week.

The Wednesday rehearsal included two video cameras, one run by Lila and the other by Peter DeHaven. When they began, Jessica was surprised to find that Randy had already memorized all his lines and that Winston already knew most of his. *I've got plenty of time to learn my lines*, Jessica told herself. *After all, I am the star*. She read her lines as if she was bored, stopping frequently to make complaints about the lights, the heat, the noise level, and the camera placement. Finally, when it was time for The Slime to kiss the heroine, she started to cough—and cough and cough.

"I think I'm coming down with a cold," she explained thickly to Mr. Bowman. Noisily, she blew her nose on a tissue.

"Funny how it came on all of a sudden," Mr. Bowman replied dryly. "Well, I don't think you should pass your germs around." Mr. Bowman grinned at Randy and Winston. "I know this will break your hearts, guys. But let's just read the lines from the kissing scenes for the next day or two and omit the action until Jessica's cold is gone."

"Too bad, Jessica," Winston joked. "You don't know what you're missing."

"Better take some cold medicine, Jessica!" Jerry yelled, and Jessica's face flamed. *Boys are so stupid!* she thought angrily.

When rehearsal was over, Mr. Bowman came over to talk to her. "I suggest that you memorize your lines right away, Jessica," he said. "Then you can start working on characterization. In fact, I'd like to see you without your script tomorrow."

Jessica tossed her hair over her shoulder. "Oh, all right," she said.

"We could do without some of the prima donna stuff, too," Colin said pointedly after Mr. Bowman had walked away.

Jessica glared at Colin. But at least she had made her point perfectly clear—*she* was the star of the show, and she demanded respect. And she had gotten out of the kissing scenes for two days in a row!

Once camera rehearsals began, Lila suddenly seemed to have forgotten that she had ever been angry at Jessica for getting the female lead. In fact, Jessica could not help but notice that Lila was going out of her way to be helpful and supportive.

"I think you're doing a marvelous job in the movie, Jessica," Lila said on Thursday during gym class. "I couldn't have done better."

"Do you really think so?" Jessica asked. She was a little surprised at Lila's compliment, but she was also gratified that her friend had recognized the truth at last.

"I do," Lila said firmly. "I take back every mean thing I said or thought about you for getting the part instead of me."

During rehearsal later that afternoon, Lila kept her camera focused on Jessica. Then right in the middle of a scene, she yelled, "Cut!" The action stopped, and everybody looked at her.

"*I'm* the one who's supposed to say 'cut,' " Colin said irritably. "What's wrong, Lila?"

Lila smiled and walked around to the other side of the stage. "Nothing's wrong," she said calmly. "I just want to make sure that Jessica has the best camera angle." She squinted through the camcorder. "There. That's a *lot* better. OK, Jessica, you can go on now."

After rehearsal, Lila offered to walk home with Jessica. "I hadn't realized what a really difficult role you have, Jessica," she said. "Especially those two kissing scenes. Randy and Winston are not the sort of guys you want to rehearse a kiss with."

Jessica pretended to sneeze. "Well," she said, "I do have this terrible cold. Even Mr. Bowman says I shouldn't rehearse the kissing scenes until I'm better."

"Of course not," Lila said sympathetically. "But you know, I was thinking. When there's a fight in the movies, the punches are faked so that nobody ever gets hurt. Why can't you fake your kisses?"

Jessica frowned doubtfully. "Fake kisses? How would I do that?"

"It's easy," Lila said. "Janet showed me. Hey, why don't you come over tonight and I'll teach you. In fact, I'll even record it on the camcorder so you can study it and see how the kisses are going to look on the screen."

Jessica hesitated. *Why is Lila on my side all of a sudden?* she wondered. *Is she up to something? Maybe she's just learned how to be a good loser.* Jessica smiled at Lila. "OK, I'll be over after dinner."

*   *   *

"You see," Lila said when Jessica got to her house that night, "you don't really kiss the other person on the mouth. You aim for a spot just *beside* the mouth. And actually, your lips never even *touch* the other person. You turn your head at an angle. That hides what you're actually doing."

"Oh," Jessica said slowly. "But there's only one problem, Lila. How can I practice fake kissing when I don't have anybody to practice with?"

"That's easy." Lila handed Jessica a pillow. "Pretend this pillow is Randy or Winston. I'll turn the camera on when you're ready."

Jessica held the pillow in her arms and looked at it doubtfully. "You're sure this will work?" she asked.

"Of course," Lila said reassuringly. She picked up the camcorder. "Just try. It's not hard."

Jessica closed her eyes. *Here goes*, she thought. *It's got to be better than kissing a nerd*. Then she gently pressed her lips to the pillow.

"No, don't kiss it, Jessica," Lila said. "Just pretend you're kissing it."

Jessica tried again, and this time she barely let her lips graze it. "How was that?" she asked.

"Not bad," Lila said. "You'll have to turn your head more to the left, though. Ready for the camera?"

"Ready," Jessica replied, and faked another

kiss in the direction of the pillow. When she was finished, she put the pillow down. "Let's look at the tape," she said eagerly.

Lila sighed. "Well, actually, we're not going to be able to see it tonight. When I got home, I found out that Dad had loaned our VCR to somebody at the office."

"OK, then," Jessica said, "I'll take the tape home and look at it on our VCR."

Lila held out the tape. "Sure," she agreed, "as long as you're willing to run the risk of Steven seeing it."

Jessica frowned. "That's a pretty big risk," she said thoughtfully. "Steven is in and out of the den all the time. I'll never be able to keep him out while I'm watching it."

"It would be safer if I kept it here," Lila said. "Our VCR will be back by Monday. You'll still have plenty of time to study your technique."

"All right. Hey, thanks for your help, Lila," Jessica said. "I really appreciate it."

Lila smiled brightly. "What are friends for?"

Eight

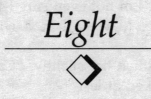

On Friday afternoon, Leslie asked Elizabeth, Maria, and Amy to come over to her house that evening.

"Sure!" Elizabeth said. "We can celebrate finishing an entire week of rehearsals!"

"And I thought we could rent a movie," Leslie suggested.

When Elizabeth had walked off, Leslie frowned. It suddenly occurred to her that renting a movie meant going to Sweet Valley Video. She had been avoiding Deirdre since the auditions. She was ashamed to tell Deirdre that she had chickened out. *Well, I can't stay away forever*, she thought. *I might as well go and get it over with.*

"Hi, Leslie," Deirdre said when Leslie came into the shop. "I haven't seen you for a while. I guess you've been busy with your movie, huh?"

"Yeah," Leslie said quietly. "I've been really busy."

Deirdre frowned. "You *did* get the part you wanted, didn't you?"

"Actually, I decided not to audition. Anyway, it's no big deal. I'm not even sure I want to be an actress anymore. Maybe I'll be a writer or something."

Deirdre studied her silently. "Can I tell you a secret?" she asked at last.

"I guess," Leslie said, struggling now to hide the tears that were brimming in her eyes.

"You know I studied acting in college," Deirdre said, and Leslie nodded. "More than anything else, I wanted to be an actress. Movies, television, theater—it didn't matter what. I started drama lessons at five, I starred in every high school play, and then I went to the drama school at the university."

"And then what happened?" Leslie asked.

"Then I went to New York, just as I'd planned, and one of my teachers helped me get an audition for a big Broadway play. When the day of the audition came, I was petrified. I went to the audition and watched the other actors who were scheduled before me. They all seemed so much more experienced than I was. So I left."

"But what happened after that?" Leslie asked.

"After that, I gave up acting entirely. I guess I lost my nerve. But I've always wondered what would have happened if I *had* auditioned that day. I've always been sorry—I mean, *really* sorry—that I didn't." Deirdre shook her head regretfully. "Trust me, Leslie. It's better to try and fail than not to try at all."

Leslie bit her lip. She knew that Deirdre was right. She should have auditioned. If she had not gotten the part, at least she would have known for sure that she was not a good actress. And maybe she *would* have gotten the part. Maybe when she was in front of the camera with Randy, she would not have been shy at all. Maybe . . . maybe. . . .

Leslie's shoulders slumped. All the maybes in the world would not change the fact that it was too late now. The auditions were over, the parts had been assigned, and the rehearsals were under way. There was nothing she could do now but feel miserable.

That evening, Elizabeth, Amy, and Maria came over to Leslie's house. Elizabeth brought some cupcakes she had baked, Amy and Maria brought soda, and after Leslie popped some popcorn, they went into the den and sat down to watch some of the tape from the class movie. Mr.

Bowman had let Elizabeth take the tape home for the weekend so the scriptwriters could study it for problems.

"I don't think we need to make any changes at all," Maria said after they had watched the tape twice. "Of course, it's a little hard to tell exactly how the finished movie will look because the actors are just walking through their roles without sets or costumes. But I still think it's great."

"Winston will be even funnier when Lois finishes making his Slime suit," Amy said. "And I think the kissing scenes will be really cute, too!"

"By the way," Leslie asked, "how's Jessica's cold?"

Elizabeth laughed. "I don't think it's very serious," she said. "She forgets all about it the minute she gets away from the camera."

"If we're finished with *The Slime That Ate Sweet Valley*," Leslie said as she passed around another bowl of popcorn, "we could watch *Private Paradise*."

"*Private Paradise* starring Dolores Dufay!" Maria said. "She's one of my favorite actresses."

"Mine, too," Elizabeth said. "It's hard to believe that Jessica actually acted with her once."

"Lucky Jessica." Leslie sighed as she put the tape into the VCR.

"Yeah." Amy laughed. "It figures that Jessica Wakefield would get a break like that!"

Elizabeth and Amy pulled up pillows and lay down on the floor, while Maria and Leslie sat on the sofa. For the next hour, their eyes were glued to the screen.

"There's no doubt about it," Maria whispered just before the final scene in the movie. "*Private Paradise* is Dolores Dufay's best film."

"Yeah," Leslie said, "and the best part is coming up."

Then, as the last scene began, the sound failed.

"Hey!" Amy exclaimed. "What happened to the sound?"

Leslie went to the VCR and fiddled with the controls. "It's not the VCR. It must be this copy of the movie. It's probably defective."

"Defective!" Amy moaned. "You mean, we won't get to hear the last scene?"

"We could lip-read," Elizabeth suggested with a laugh. "Look. Right now the heroine is saying something like, 'I love you, darling.'"

Leslie pushed the rewind button and replayed the line. "No, she's saying, 'I've always loved you, darling. And I always will, no matter what happens—and no matter whether *you* care or not.'"

"Oh, yeah?" Amy asked, leaning forward. "And what's *he* saying?"

"He doesn't believe her," Leslie replied. "He's

saying 'It's only in the movies that love is forever. In real life, love comes and goes. You'll find someone else.' " Leslie stopped, her face reddening. "I'm sorry, I didn't mean to—"

"Go on, Leslie," Maria urged. "What does she say next?"

Then Leslie recited the final scene, playing both parts. As she spoke the lines, she put meaning into every phrase. When the scene was over and the movie ended, Elizabeth, Amy, and Maria let out a collective sigh.

"Boy, am I glad you knew all those lines, Leslie," Amy said.

"How *did* you know all the lines?" Elizabeth asked. "It must have taken a lot of work to memorize that entire scene."

"It wasn't a lot of work," Leslie said modestly. "At least, I didn't think so."

"Don't give me that," Maria said. "Memorizing both the male and female parts took *real work*. And you played the scene really well. Leslie, you're an *incredibly* talented actress!"

"Do you really think so?" Leslie whispered incredulously. "That means a *lot* to me, coming from you, Maria."

"Absolutely," Maria said. "Leslie, *why* didn't you audition for the lead in our movie? You're a much better actress than Jessica." Maria smiled at Elizabeth. "Sorry, Elizabeth, but it's true—in my opinion, anyway. I've watched Jessica rehearse for the last couple of days, and she acts as if she's totally bored with the whole thing."

"You're right, Maria," Elizabeth said. "Leslie, what *really* happened on the day of the auditions? Why didn't you come?"

Leslie hesitated a minute. "Actually," she said slowly, "I did come. I was sitting a few rows behind everyone else. It was dark in the auditorium, you know," she added uncomfortably. "I don't think anybody saw me."

"But if you were there," Amy asked, "why didn't you come up when Mr. Bowman called on you? Didn't you want the part after all?"

"Yes, I wanted the part," Leslie said. "I wanted it more than anything."

"Was it because of Lila and Ellen?" Elizabeth asked.

"Partly," Leslie replied in a low voice. "I heard what they said about me, and it really hurt. But there was something else, too. I guess I might as well tell you the whole thing. You see, Mr. Bowman assigned Randy Mason to play opposite me. And I . . . well, I just didn't think I could do the scene with him because—well, because I *like* Randy."

"Listen, Leslie," Maria said with a grin, "I know exactly what you're talking about. Last year I got this job working with Jason Dare in an ice-cream commercial. But I had this terrible crush on him, and it made me feel so shy, I could hardly open my mouth! I mean, here I was dressed as a dish of ice cream, and I felt like melting into a little puddle!" She giggled. "It probably wouldn't have gone over big with the director."

"You mean, something like that can happen to someone as experienced as *you*?" Leslie asked.

Maria laughed. "Are you kidding? It happens to *everybody*. Hollywood is full of stars who lose their cool when they get near somebody they like a lot."

"But what do you *do* in a situation like that?" Leslie asked. "I mean, how do you handle it?"

"You *act*. You play the role and forget about how you *feel*. That's what makes you a pro."

"I'll bet that's Jessica's problem," Amy said. "She's letting her feelings influence her performance."

"Right," Maria said. "And that's bad for our movie."

"I really wish you had auditioned, Leslie," Elizabeth said.

"I wish now that I had," Leslie said wistfully. "But life isn't like watching a video. I mean, you can't push the rewind button and have another chance. But hey, it means a lot to me to know that you guys think I'm good. Maybe I'll have more courage for the *next* movie we make."

"Courage is the most important thing you can have," Maria said.

"No," Leslie said with a smile. "*Friends* are the most important thing you can have!"

Late that same Friday afternoon, Lila had announced that she was having a few friends over that evening for a party. "We might even look at some of the videotapes I've been making," she added. "Can you come, Jessica? I've invited Aaron."

"Sure," Jessica said eagerly. And then she frowned.

"Hey, wait a minute, Lila. I thought you said that someone in your father's office had borrowed your VCR. That was why I couldn't look at my fake-kissing scene last night—remember?"

"I *did* say that someone had borrowed our VCR because someone *had*," Lila answered. "But he returned it."

Jessica looked closely at Lila. "Oh," she said skeptically.

"It's perfect, Jess," Lila continued quickly. "After everyone leaves tonight, you can hang around and watch your tape. If you want, we can reshoot it so that you get *more* practice."

Jessica studied her friend, and all she saw was Lila's smiling, open face. "OK, I'll be there. And thanks, Lila."

Lila smiled brightly. "Don't mention it, Jess. I'm sure you'd do the same for me."

When Jessica got to Lila's house that evening, she was surprised to see that Lila had invited more than just a few friends. Almost everybody she knew was there, including all of the Unicorns, and Bruce Patman and his crowd. For a while everyone played Ping-Pong in the Fowlers' recreation room, danced to Lila's stereo, and munched snacks out on the patio. And then when they were bored with partying, Lila gathered them all in the Fowlers' TV room and turned on the giant-screen TV, which was hooked up to the VCR.

"I thought everyone would like to see some of the videos I've been making," she said. "After all, some of you here are *stars*."

Jessica sat down on the sofa next to Aaron. "Maybe Lila will show some of our rehearsal videos," she said.

Lila pushed the start button, and a bright image came to life on the screen. "Hey," Ellen said indignantly, "that's the tape you shot when we went shopping last Saturday. I thought you said we'd see it in private!"

"I lied," Lila said with a laugh.

There on the giant screen was Ellen, trapped in her too-tight pullover, red-faced and embarrassed. Then there was Jessica, with her blouse buttoned crookedly, and Mandy, trying to lick the maraschino cherry juice off her nose.

"Hey, Lila," Mandy protested, "this isn't fair! You promised!"

"Be a good sport, Mandy," Lila replied. "These scenes are *so* funny! Wait until you see the sequence that's coming up. It's a riot!"

What came onto the giant screen next was Aaron somersaulting head-over-heels off his skateboard. And there was Jessica, scrambling down into the drainage ditch to rescue him, shrieking hysterically for an ambulance. When she put her arms around him and Aaron pushed her away, Bruce roared with laughter. "What's the matter, Dallas?" he asked. "Florence Nightingale a little too close for comfort?"

Aaron's face was flaming, and Jessica felt hers getting red, too. But the crowd was paying no attention to them. They were laughing at a shot of Ellen, who had tried to roller-skate and eat a frozen yogurt cone at the same time and had ended up on her rear in a prickly cactus.

"Hey, your face is really red, Ellen," Charlie cackled.

"That's not all that's red," Bruce added.

Then the crowd roared as Belinda, batting for the softball team, struck out so hard on a third strike that she fell right into the arms of the catcher.

And then there was a lull in the action. "I think you'll all get a laugh out of the next sequence," Lila said. "It's the star of our sixth-grade movie, showing her stuff."

"Hey, Jess," Aaron said. "That means you."

Lila laughed loudly. "That's right. And can you believe it? Our famous star is making out with a *pillow!*"

Jessica sucked in her breath. There on the giant screen, for everybody to see, was the video that Lila had made the night before. Jessica watched herself holding the sofa cushion and kissing it—except that she wasn't really kissing it. Her fake kisses were clearly, embarrassingly fake. *How could I have been so dumb!* she thought desperately. *I can't believe I fell for Lila's trick!*

"Hey, Aaron," Charlie called, "is *that* the way Jessica does it?"

Jessica saw Aaron scrunch down beside her. He didn't say a word.

"Well, if *that's* the way she kisses," Bruce yelled, "give me a pillow instead!"

Aaron still refused to answer, and his ears had turned bright red. Jessica was so mortified that she wished she could die, right on the spot. She wasn't the star. She was everybody's idea of a great big joke!

When the video was over, Lila came over to Jessica. "If I'd known how much the video was going to embarrass you, Jessica," she said, "I *never* would have shown it. I just thought it was funny, that's all."

"Funny!" Jessica said angrily. "It wasn't funny. It was humiliating! Utterly humiliating!"

Lila shook her head. "Gosh, Jessica, if you're humiliated by kissing a pillow, just think how awful you'll feel when you kiss two of the biggest nerds ever born, in front of the entire school!"

Jessica tried to think of some sort of rebuttal, but she knew that Lila was right.

"It's really too bad you got that part, Jessica," Lila continued. "But I guess there's nothing you can do about it now, is there? *Is* there?"

Nine

◇

"I quit!" Jessica shouted Monday morning in class.

"Well, Jessica, if you don't like the part, you can't do it justice," Mr. Bowman said simply. "So by all means, bow out now."

Why can't Mr. Bowman at least pretend to be upset? Jessica thought. *He sounds as if he's glad to be rid of me!*

"I've suspected since the first rehearsal that your heart really isn't in this role, Jessica." Mr. Bowman continued. "It's actually better for the movie if we replace you with somebody who really *wants* the role, even if she doesn't have your experience."

"I see," was all Jessica could say.

"Isn't it great?" Amy exclaimed to Elizabeth after class. "Now Leslie can try out for the lead!"

"Yeah," Maria said. "But we actually have to talk her into trying out!"

"Leslie Forsythe?" Lila asked as she joined them. "Oh, she'd be perfect as the female lead! Randy's a geek, Winston's a jerk, and Leslie's a mouse. They'll make a perfect team!"

"Right," Ellen agreed with a giggle. "A perfect trio of nerds."

"You two," Amy interrupted, "are absolutely the most despicable pair of—"

"Actually," Leslie said as she joined them, "I think Lila and Ellen might be right." She lifted her chin defiantly, and her eyes sparked fire. "Winston and Randy and I *are* pretty well matched. We're all serious actors!"

Elizabeth smiled. "Then you've decided to try out for the role! Leslie, that's *terrific!*"

"Well," Lila said with a smirk, "in that case, I think we should rename the movie *The Geeks That Ate Sweet Valley!*"

Leslie was not nearly as confident on the inside as she tried to appear on the outside. When she thought of acting opposite Randy, her mouth still got dry and cottony. *But this time*, she told herself as she headed for the auditorium after school, *I'm not going to let being scared stop me. I have to show Elizabeth and Amy and Maria and Deirdre that I'm really the actress they think I am. But most of all, I have to show myself.*

The auditorium was almost empty. Two other sixth-grade girls tried out for the part, playing opposite Randy. With Elizabeth sitting on one side of her and Maria and Amy on the other, Leslie watched them audition, trying to pretend she wasn't scared. When it was finally her turn, Elizabeth squeezed one hand and Maria squeezed the other.

"We're rooting for you," Elizabeth whispered.

"Don't forget," Maria added. "It's OK to feel like melting on the inside, but stay cool on the outside, like a pro."

Leslie nodded, went up onto the stage, and took the script Mr. Bowman handed her. "I'm glad you could make it this time, Leslie," he said.

"I am, too," Randy said shyly. "I was hoping you'd try out."

"You were?" Leslie asked, amazed.

Randy nodded shyly.

Leslie smiled, then turned to Mr. Bowman. "OK, I'm ready."

And from that moment on, it was easy. Randy swung into the auditioning script with confidence. " 'I've told you over and over again, Amanda,' " he said firmly, " 'but you never hear me. Why don't you just shut up and listen for a change? The truth is that—' "

" 'Now, it's *your* turn to listen to *me*,' " Leslie interrupted furiously. " 'The truth is that *you're* a pain, Bob. A total pain!' "

" 'You think so?' " Randy replied, raising his eyebrows. " 'Since when are you an authority on who's a pain, Amanda?' "

" 'Since right *now*!' " Leslie replied. She had forgotten about the audience. And she found herself acting the way she always knew, deep in her heart, that she could. And it was *fun!*

When Leslie and Randy finished the scene, there was a moment of silence. Then Elizabeth, Amy, and Maria began to applaud, and a moment later, Mr. Bowman announced that the part was hers. But it was not until her friends were congratulating her that Leslie let herself believe that her secret dream was actually coming true at last.

"What about kissing The Slime?" Amy teased as they left the auditorium together. "Doesn't that bother you?"

"Or kissing Randy?" Maria asked, her eyes twinkling.

"Yeah," Elizabeth asked. "Aren't you nervous?"

Leslie tossed her head. "Not at all. All great actresses have to make sacrifices for their careers!"

*   *   *

With Randy's help, Leslie memorized her part almost immediately and filming began on location in Leslie's basement, which Charlie and Todd had fixed up to look as spooky as possible.

"There are *bats* down there," Lila complained to Mr. Bowman on Tuesday as they were getting ready to film. "And cobwebs. And who knows what else." She shuddered. "Maybe even snakes."

"Lila," Elizabeth said, rolling her eyes, "there are no *snakes* in Leslie's basement."

"And the bats aren't real," Pete assured her.

"Are you sure?" Lila asked dubiously.

"Yeah, I'm sure," Pete said as he pulled a black rubber bat out of his pocket and dangled it in Lila's face. Lila shrank back. "See? Totally fake. There's nothing to be scared about."

"OK, gang!" Mr. Bowman called. "We're ready for today's shooting. Let's get the cameras down here."

Reluctantly, Lila agreed to take her camera into the basement. But as soon as she had gotten set up, she jumped, gave a loud screech, and nearly dropped her camcorder.

"What's wrong now, Lila?" Mr. Bowman asked.

"Spiders!" Lila shrieked hysterically. "There are *spiders* down here!"

Mr. Bowman sat on a stool in the corner, his script in his hand. "They won't hurt you, Lila.

Let's try it from the top of scene three," he said. "We'll run through the scene a couple of times, and then shoot for real."

Colin clapped his hands. "Quiet on the set!" he called. The crew fell silent as the lights came on and Caroline, playing the grandmother, felt her way down the stairs. She wore a gray wig, a shapeless housedress, and an old-fashioned apron.

" 'Is anybody down here?' " Caroline called, her voice quavery and fearful. " 'I thought I heard somebody moving around. Is somebody here?' "

At that moment, Winston stepped out of the shadows under the stairs, wearing The Slime costume—a loose, green, baglike thing made out of flexible plastic and stuffed with foam peanuts.

" 'Eek!' " Caroline screeched when she saw The Slime.

" 'Ah, lunch at last!' " The Slime said happily. " 'A tasty morsel, if a little on the mature side.' " He reached for Caroline, and his green costume enveloped her.

"Cut!" Mr. Bowman called. "That was good, Caroline. Only the next time, drag out the scream a little more. That's not a harmless little mouse you're seeing—it's The Slime! He's going to eat all of Sweet Valley if he's not stopped!"

"Yeah," Winston cried. "I'm hungry. Where's

the sister? And the principal?" He rubbed his slimy hands together. "Especially the principal!"

Jessica plodded into the cafeteria on Thursday, looking glum. "What's wrong?" Lila asked.

"I hate to sew," Jessica complained. She held out her finger to display a huge Band-Aid. "I keep poking myself with the needle. Why did Mr. Bowman have to make *me* help Lois sew the costumes?"

"It's too bad that Mr. Bowman couldn't have found a better job for you," Ellen said sympathetically.

"Yeah," Lila agreed. "Something more in line with your real talents—like kissing pillows!"

"Very funny, Lila," Jessica snapped. *Just you wait, Lila Fowler*, she thought as she followed Lila and Ellen toward the Unicorn table. *You'll get yours!*

"Working with Lois must be a total drag," Ellen said as they sat down. "She's such a wimp."

Jessica sneezed. "I can't think of anyone wimpier. And not only that," she added tragically, "I think I'm allergic to the foam peanuts we use to stuff Winston's costume."

"Wait a minute. I thought you and Lois were finished with his costume," Ellen said. "I mean, Winston's been wearing it already."

"We are finished," Jessica replied with a sigh. "But the material keeps ripping apart, which means that I have to always be ready with a needle and thread to sew it back up again."

"Poor Jessica," Lila said pityingly. "You know, I'm surprised at how good Leslie is in your old role. I'll bet you regret giving up the part."

"Not in the slightest," Jessica said with a toss of her head.

"Hey, what did you tell your parents about having dropped out, Jess?" Ellen asked slyly.

"I told them the truth. I told them I thought I just couldn't do justice to the role. And that rehearsals were taking away from my study time."

Lila grinned but did not answer, and in a minute the rest of the Unicorns joined them. Jessica pretended to listen to the loud chatter that surrounded her, but all the while she was really trying to figure out how to get revenge on Lila for showing everyone the video of her and the pillow. She had already come up with half a dozen schemes, but they were all too complicated. And anyway, time was getting short. The class was taping now, and when they were finished, Pete and a few others would edit it, and next Monday, it would be shown to the entire school. If Jessica was going to get even with Lila, she knew she had better think fast.

Jessica was just getting up from the table

when she caught sight of Pete launching a spitball at the unsuspecting back of a boy a few feet away. Jessica narrowed her eyes. How could she have forgotten? Pete was a natural-born trickster. Since they had started the movie, he had been too busy for pranks, but maybe, just maybe, if she could get Pete to help her . . .

Ten

◇

That weekend, Mandy held a sleep-over for the sixth-grade Unicorns to celebrate the end of the taping of *The Slime That Ate Sweet Valley*.

Ellen had brought a couple of new video-tapes, Belinda brought a stack of movie and rock magazines, and Jessica brought two games and a big batch of chocolate chip cookies. Lila brought her video camera.

"OK, everybody," Mandy announced suddenly, "it's time for the Weird Pajama Contest I told you we'd have."

Everybody dived for their overnight bags. Belinda's weird pajamas turned out to be an old Ranger T-shirt and a pair of baseball pants. Ellen's was a slinky black lace nightgown that belonged to her mother. Mandy's was a hospital gown from her stay in the hospital after her cancer operation.

Jessica had borrowed her weird pajamas from her father—an old blue shirt with the sleeves rolled up. And Lila wore a knee-length purple T-shirt with a Unicorn painted on it, and the words I'M THE STAR! written across the front in big red letters.

"Those pajamas are the best, Lila," Jessica said as she handed Lila the grand prize—an expensive European oatmeal facial mask that Ellen had gotten from her mother.

"Thanks," Lila said proudly. "I think I'll put it on right now."

"And here's the other prize," Ellen said. "It's a special hair-setting lotion loaded with conditioners. I've brought some curlers, too. Let's put the lotion on and roll up your hair when you start your facial."

The Unicorns settled down to wait for Lila's facial mask to dry and for the hair-setting lotion to do its work. "You know," Jessica said with a sigh, "I guess I *am* sorry I gave up the starring role. There's a wonderful magic to being on camera." She turned to Ellen, who had played the part of a victim in the movie. "Don't you think so, Ellen?"

"Oh, yes," she agreed earnestly. "There's nothing like being in front of the camera."

"I agree," Belinda said. "I could *feel* it, even

though my role was very small. The camera makes you feel really different.''

''Different?'' Lila asked skeptically. ''What's so *different* about being in front of a camera?''

''I don't know what it is,'' Mandy said, shaking her head. ''But there *is* a magic about acting. You're in a whole different world. Nothing is more exciting—*nothing*.''

''Poor Lila,'' Jessica said sympathetically. ''I guess you really can't know what we're talking about, can you? You've never *been* in front of a camera.''

''That's right,'' Mandy said. ''It's a feeling we can't describe to you, Lila. It can only be *experienced*.''

''Yeah, I really feel sorry for you, Lila,'' Ellen added. ''You're the only sixth-grade Unicorn who isn't somehow involved in acting.''

''You're right,'' Lila muttered. ''And it's kind of ironic, because I'm a very good actress. In fact, I'm probably the best actress in this room.''

''You probably are,'' Ellen agreed heartily.

Jessica snapped her fingers. ''You know, Lila, you could experience a little of that magic right here and now. After all, we *do* have a camera.''

''That's right, Jessica!'' Mandy exclaimed. ''Lila could do a scene for us now and show us her talent!''

"But we haven't got any film," Lila objected. "The tape that's in there now has only a few seconds left on it."

"That's OK," Jessica said easily. "I'll just pretend to film you. You'll still get the feel of what it's like to be in front of the camera."

"OK," Lila said. "Now I'll have a chance to show you guys how a *real* actress plays a scene."

"What scene do you want to play?" Belinda asked.

"The balcony scene from *Romeo and Juliet*," Lila said. "I know it by heart."

"That's a great idea!" Mandy said enthusiastically.

"You can play Romeo if you want to, Mandy," Lila said. "Don't you know the part from the Drama Club auditions?"

"Yeah, but I'd just detract from the experience, Lila. I'll get you something to represent Romeo so that you can experience a solo performance."

"How about a dust mop?" Ellen suggested.

"Yeah," Lila said. "That'll work. But I have to get this goop off my face first."

"No," Jessica said hurriedly. "I mean, it hasn't had a chance to do what it's supposed to do yet. You wouldn't want to waste it by taking it off too soon, would you?"

"I guess not," Lila agreed. "But let's at least do something with my hair."

While Mandy went in search of a dust mop, Ellen and Belinda took the curlers out of Lila's hair. Meanwhile, Jessica took the old tape out of the camcorder and slipped in a brand-new one she had brought with her.

When Lila was ready, Jessica pushed the on button, and the camera whirred. "Action!" she called.

Lila began to speak. At first, she was a little self-conscious, but then she launched into the passion of the scene. When she was finished, the Unicorns applauded.

"No doubt about it—you really *are* a star, Lila," Mandy said.

"It's too bad that *everybody* can't see what an extraordinary talent you have," Jessica said.

"Oh, I'm sure I'll get my chance someday," Lila said confidently. "Talent has a way of popping out, you know. When you're as naturally talented as I am, you can't keep it hidden for long."

"Oh, absolutely," Jessica agreed with a little smile.

On Monday, the sixth, seventh, and eighth graders, as well as the parents of those who were involved in the making of *The Slime That Ate Sweet Valley*, gathered in the auditorium for the showing.

Elizabeth, Jessica, and Todd sat together in the front row. Elizabeth turned around to look at the crowd. She waved to her parents, who were several rows behind them, and then she saw another familiar face and nudged Leslie, who was sitting on her left. "Look, Leslie!" she said excitedly. "It's Deirdre."

"I know," Leslie said as she turned to wave. "I invited her."

"Leslie's cooler than any of us!" Todd said.

Elizabeth smiled. "Yeah, Leslie. You don't look at all nervous about the showing of the movie."

"That's because I *know* we all made a great movie," Leslie responded. "Hey, here comes Mr. Bowman."

Mr. Bowman got up onstage and welcomed the crowd. He told them a little bit about how the movie had been planned and created, and why such a project was a good one for an English class. Then he asked Aaron to turn down the lights, and Pete started the VCR. The wide-screen TV flickered on.

Elizabeth had not seen the final edited version, so she was not sure exactly what to expect. She was surprised to see the caption COMING SOON

TO A THEATER NEAR YOU flash across the screen. And she was even more surprised to see the words A TRIBUTE TO LILA FOWLER, THE GREATEST ACTRESS OF ALL TIME appear, accompanied by the theme melody from *Gone With the Wind*. A puzzled murmur rose up from the sixth graders. Some of the seventh and eighth graders laughed.

"What's this?" Leslie whispered.

"I don't know anything about it," Elizabeth answered. "Do you, Jess?"

"Wait and see," Jessica said mysteriously.

The theme music swelled louder, and suddenly Lila appeared on the screen, wearing a purple shirt with a Unicorn and the words I'M THE STAR! plastered across the front. Her face was covered with something that looked suspiciously like oatmeal. And then she was clutching a dust mop and smothering it with kisses. " 'Oh, Romeo,' " she murmured, " 'wherefore art thou, Romeo.' "

Bruce yelled, "Right here, Lila!" and the audience roared as Lila delivered the rest of the scene with great passion. Finally, she looked longingly into the shaggy head of the dust mop and whispered, " 'Parting is such sweet sorrow.' " The music swelled again, and Lila's image faded.

The audience continued to howl with laughter. "Wasn't it wonderful?" Jessica gasped. "Wasn't that absolutely the most stunning dramatic performance you've ever seen in your whole, entire life? A dust mop! Lila Fowler making mad, passionate love to a dust mop!"

"She doesn't look as if she's in a very romantic mood right now," Todd said. "Look."

From where she sat, Elizabeth could see that Lila Fowler, The Greatest Actress of All Time, was not amused. Her lips were pressed tightly together, her face was as red as a fire engine, and her hands were clenched in her lap.

The audience quickly quieted as *The Slime That Ate Sweet Valley* began. The movie was an enormous hit, and when it was over, Deirdre hurried up to Leslie and Elizabeth. "Congratulations, Leslie," she said. "You were a sensation!" She handed Leslie a bouquet of red roses and a card that read: "To a great star—and a courageous person."

Leslie's eyes were shining. "Do you really think so?" she whispered.

"Yes, I do," Deirdre said firmly. "You've even inspired me. I'm going to get back into acting. I've already signed up for an open call in L.A."

As Elizabeth looked on, Leslie threw her arms around Deirdre and gave her a hug. "That's terrific, Deirdre. Hey, maybe someday we can act together!"

"It would be a privilege," Deirdre said.

*　　*　　*

Later, after all the parents had left, the Unicorns, except for Lila, gathered for lunch. For once, they did not eat at the Unicorner. Instead, they joined Elizabeth, Amy, Leslie, and Maria to talk about their successful movie.

"Before anybody says anything about *The Slime*," Maria began, "I want to know how that film of Lila got onto our videotape!"

All eyes swung to Jessica.

"Why is everybody looking at me?" Jessica asked innocently.

"Because it was your idea," Mandy said.

"Yeah, but I couldn't have done it if you and Belinda and Ellen hadn't helped," Jessica said. "And Pete Stone."

"Pete?" Leslie asked. "What did *he* have to do with it?"

"Maybe you'd better start at the beginning, Jessica," Belinda said.

Jessica nodded. "Mandy and Belinda and Ellen and I were pretty fed up with Lila taking embarrassing films of us with her camcorder," she said. "So we decided to give her a dose of her own medicine. That video you saw was taken at Mandy's sleep-over last Saturday."

"I can't believe you actually got Lila to do all that silly stuff," Elizabeth said. "Didn't she realize you were taping her?"

"No." Ellen laughed. "Lila thought the camcorder was empty and that we were just pretending."

"But I still don't understand how you got Lila's act into our movie," Leslie asked.

Jessica giggled. "Do you remember the ghost of the English classroom?"

"Yeah. The person who was playing all those tricks on Mr. Bowman, back before we started the movie," Elizabeth said.

"Right," Jessica said. "The ghost was Pete. I know because I caught him. Well, when I came up with the idea of taping Lila, Pete and I made a deal. In return for my not telling Mr. Bowman that Pete was responsible for the tricks, Pete agreed to edit Lila's act into our movie."

"You blackmailed Pete into doing your dirty work?" Amy exclaimed.

Jessica smiled modestly. "Yeah. Pretty smart of me, huh? But it wasn't really blackmail," she explained. "Pete was glad to cooperate. He was pretty sick of Lila, too."

"Poor Lila!" Maria said.

"Lila got what she wanted most of all," Jessica said.

"What's that?" Amy asked.

Jessica grinned. "Stardom!"

Jessica reached for a second piece of chocolate cake that night at dinner.

"I wonder what Aaron would say if he saw the way his *girlfriend* eats!" Steven said.

Jessica stuck her tongue out at her brother. "For your information, Steven, Aaron has seen me eat plenty of times. And *no one* is ever going to tell me not to eat chocolate cake!"

"I wouldn't talk if I were you, Steven," Elizabeth said. "You're the *vacuum* that ate Sweet Valley!"

"Yeah, but I'm a guy," Steven protested.

"And I can't eat what I like because I'm a girl?" Jessica demanded.

"I can't believe you, Steven! You are *so* sexist," Elizabeth said angrily.

"OK, you guys," Mr. Wakefield said. "Let's keep it down."

"But, *Dad*, can't I even defend myself?" Steven argued.

"No, for two reasons," his father replied. "Number one, you're totally in the wrong. . . ."

"And number two," Mrs. Wakefield continued, "your father and I would like to at least *pretend* that we're a well-behaved family capable of having a civilized meal together."

"All right," Steven grumbled.

"This trip to Mexico is sounding better all the time!" Mr. Wakefield laughed.

"Are you definitely going?" Jessica asked excitedly.

"*Almost* definitely," Mrs. Wakefield answered.

"Will you bring us back lots of souvenirs?" Elizabeth teased.

"Tons," her father said.

"And you'll let us stay by ourselves?"

Both Mr. and Mrs. Wakefield laughed. "We'll see," Mrs. Wakefield said.

Will Jessica, Elizabeth, and Steven be allowed to stay home alone? Find out in Sweet Valley Twins and Friends #54, **THE BIG PARTY WEEKEND.**

The most exciting story ever in Sweet Valley history

FRANCINE
PASCAL'S

SWEET
VALLEY
Saga

THE SWEET VALLEY SAGA tells the incredible story of the lives and times of five generations of brave and beautiful young women who were Jessica and Elizabeth's ancestors. Their story is the story of America: from the danger of the pioneering days to the glamour of the roaring nineties, the sacrifice and romance of World War II to the rebelliousness of the Sixties, right up to the present-day Sweet Valley. A dazzling novel of unforgettable lives and love both lost and won, THE SWEET VALLEY SAGA is Francine Pascal's most memorable, exciting, and wonderful Sweet Valley book ever.

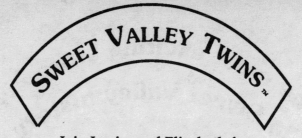

SWEET VALLEY TWINS ™

Join Jessica and Elizabeth for
big adventure in exciting
SWEET VALLEY TWINS SUPER EDITIONS
and **SWEET VALLEY TWINS CHILLERS.**

☐ **#1: CLASS TRIP** 15588-1/$3.50
☐ **#2: HOLIDAY MISCHIEF** 15641-1/$3.50
☐ **#3: THE BIG CAMP SECRET** 15707-8/$3.50
☐ **SWEET VALLEY TWINS SUPER SUMMER
FUN BOOK by Laurie Pascal Wenk**
15816-3/$3.50/3.95

Elizabeth shares her favorite summer projects &
Jessica gives you pointers on parties. Plus:
fashion tips, space to record your favorite
summer activities, quizzes, puzzles, a summer
calendar, photo album, scrapbook, address book
& more!

CHILLERS

☐ **#1: THE CHRISTMAS GHOST** 15767-1/$3.50
☐ **#2: THE GHOST IN THE GRAVEYARD**
15801-5/$3.50
☐ **#3: THE CARNIVAL GHOST** 15859-7/$2.95